SOULLESS AT SUNSET

Last Witch Standing, Book 1

DEANNA CHASE

Bayou Moon Press, LLC

About This Book

From New York Times bestselling author, Deanna Chase, comes the first book in the Last Witch Standing series featuring the badass witch, Phoebe Kilsen.

Trouble is brewing in New Orleans. Shifters are moving in and vampires are being picked off in record numbers. And vampire hunter Phoebe Kilsen is right in the middle of the war.

When Phoebe's best friend goes missing along with the consort of the most powerful vampire in New Orleans, Phoebe betrays her heart and her shifter partner by teaming up with the one vampire she's never trusted. They say all is fair in love and war, but Phoebe is putting it all on the line and she's not at all sure she'll make it out alive.

Chapter One

"*D*amn, Kilsen," a bald vampire leaning against the balcony railing drawled. "If I didn't know better, I'd say you were actively looking to be turned."

I let my gaze sweep over Liam Quats, one of Eadric Allcot's vampires. He was short and stocky with a bit of a potbelly, wearing skinny jeans, a red vest, and a green velvet jacket. My shimmering silver gown was a lot more appropriate for the gala going on inside. This guy looked like he'd stepped off the pages of a cookie advertisement. "And if I didn't know better, I'd say you were impersonating a Keebler elf."

His amused expression turned to a scowl and hatred blazed back at me. "Why do you always have to be a bitch? No wonder you're always panting after that mutt."

I followed his gaze through the double doors into the large ballroom as his stare landed on Dax Marrok, the handsome, dark-haired shifter who was my former lover. He was my current partner at the Arcane—the paranormal investigation agency we both worked for. We were part of the secret Void branch where we hunted rogue vampires. Too bad Liam wasn't on my list of assholes to apprehend. Though I was certain that if I looked hard enough, I'd find something to pin on him. He was slimier than most.

"You jealous, Liam?" I trailed two fingers down my neck, stopping at my pulse. "Think you'd like to get your fangs in me... again?"

His dark eyes started to glow gold as he stared at my neck, practically drooling. "Fangs aren't the only thing I'd like to get in you."

I reached out and grabbed a fistful of his vest and yanked him up until his toes were dragging on the ground. He let out a snarl and I snarled back, "Don't ever call me a bitch again, got it?"

His didn't—couldn't—move a muscle as his eyes blazed with fury. "What the fuck did you do to me?"

My snarl morphed into a self-satisfied smile. The paralyzing spell was definitely working. And there was no better vamp to test it out on than Liam Quats. "Feel that, Liam? Like how you're helpless, unable to fight back?"

"Let. Me. Go. Bitch!"

I tsked. "Didn't I already tell you to never call me a bitch again? You're a slow learner. This is just payback for that little stunt you pulled last month." Hatred burned in my gut as I recalled his fangs sinking into my shoulder, rendering me momentarily paralyzed before my magic kicked in and I blasted the little fucker unconscious. He'd been trying to protect the vampire I was apprehending for feeding from an unwilling human. "If you ever bite me or anyone else without permission again, I'll stake your ass, understood?"

"Phoebe?" a soft voice called from the doorway. "Problem?"

I glanced over at my best friend, Willow Rhoswen. She was standing in the open doorway, her strawberry-blond hair swept back and her blue eyes clouded with concern. I shook my head. "Not on my end." Turning my attention back to Liam, I cocked my head to the side. "How about you? Do we have a problem we need to work out?"

"You're crazy," he said, his tone icy and laced with venom. "I already paid my debt to the Arcane."

"True, but you still owed me." Thanks to the influence of Eadric Allcot, the most powerful vampire in New Orleans, the Arcane had let Liam off with just a fine and a warning. Usually vampires had to serve time for attacking an agent, but Allcot had information the Arcane wanted. No doubt a trade had been made. But no one had consulted me, and I was still pissed as hell.

I shrugged one shoulder, then tossed him backward. He landed on both feet but stumbled and awkwardly crashed into a hanging fern that sent him sprawling to the ground. Laughing, I shook my head and sashayed back into the benefit ball, linking my arm with Willow's as I went.

"Was that necessary?" she asked, her transparent fairy wings fluttering in slight agitation.

"Yes. He was being a douche."

"Phoebe…" She sighed. "Can't we just get through one event without an altercation?"

"I'm gonna say probably not." I gave the fairy a bright smile. "But since we've gotten that out of the way, hopefully the rest of the evening will be uneventful."

She snorted. "Right. Because 'uneventful' is definitely the

term I'd use to describe your evenings when vamps are around."

"It's not my fault most of them are assholes." I grabbed a flute of champagne from a passing tray.

"They're not all bad," she said, following my lead.

I clinked my glass with hers and ignored her comment. She was right. They weren't all bad. Unfortunately, the ones who worked for Allcot had proven otherwise with one hundred percent accuracy. When it came right down to it, they always rejected any shred of ethics in order to serve their leader. And tonight the ball was hosted by Allcot and his merry family of vamps, which was why I'd accepted the invitation to attend. Someone needed to keep an eye on their sorry asses.

"Forget Liam," I said. "Tonight is your night. Don't let anything ruin it. Not even me."

Willow took a sip of her champagne and smiled at me. "You could never ruin my night."

We both knew that was a lie. Before Willow had gotten married and left the Arcane, she'd been my partner. She had a unique ability that let her feel when a vampire was around, which was enormously helpful when tracking the clever ones. But she'd recently left the agency to focus on her marriage and starting a family. I glanced down at her flat belly, wondering just how soon we'd be seeing a little fae make an appearance in our lives.

Her gaze followed mine and she chuckled, apparently reading my mind as she said, "We have big plans later tonight. I'm testing a new herbal recipe designed to encourage fertility. I'm calling it Some Like It Hot Chocolate."

I rolled my eyes. "Seems like tequila shots are what worked for most of my college girlfriends."

"If that worked for us, we'd already be pregnant." Willow came to a stop next to her husband and placed a light hand on his back to let him know we were there. But I was willing to bet Talisen knew exactly where Willow was every second they'd been here, considering we were surrounded by vampires. He automatically reached for her, wrapping a protective arm around her waist.

Jesus, they were gorgeous. It was almost obscene just how blessed they were in the genetics department. The fae species has an ethereal quality about them that makes them appear incandescent. Tall and slender with glowing skin, they were almost painful to look at sometimes. Me, on the other hand? It wasn't that I was disadvantaged in the looks department, but I was the gritty sort with dark hair, black eyes, and all of five feet two inches tall. No one was ever going to hire me as a cover model. Not that I'd want the job anyway. I was too busy kicking vampire ass for anything else.

"Phoebs," Talisen said, smiling at me. "You clean up nice."

I glanced down at my sequined silver dress and exposed cleavage. "It isn't too much?"

He chuckled. "This is a gala hosted by Allcot. You could be wearing a clear plastic-wrap dress and it wouldn't be too much."

Proving his point, Pandora, Allcot's consort, strolled by wearing a see-through, lacy black bustier and a skirt that had a slit up to her hip.

"Damn, Wil," I said to my friend. "You look downright conservative in your green velvet dress."

She smoothed the formfitting, off-the-shoulder number

and nodded. "Someone needs to be the grown-up in the room."

Considering she was the host of this fundraiser to benefit a new supernatural hospital in the city and would have her picture splashed all over the local papers in the morning, she'd chosen well. Everyone else, vampires and shifters alike, appeared to be trying to one-up each other in the outrageous department. So much female skin was showing it was starting to look like a Victoria's Secret party.

"When does the auction start?" I asked Willow.

"In about fifteen minutes." She grabbed a crab puff from a passing tray and popped it into her mouth.

I raised my glass in a toast. "May their wallets be as loose as their inhibitions." As Willow laughed at me, I waved and strolled across the room, stopping only when I was side by side with Dax.

His hand landed on the small of my back, sending an electric shock of heat straight up my spine. I fought to stay perfectly still, to ignore what his touch did to me, while he continued to discuss the state of New Orleans football with a couple of young shifters. Dax and I had engaged in a short-lived, smokin'-hot affair a few months back, but I'd abruptly called it quits shortly after I'd learned he was my new partner at the Void. Dating your partner isn't a good idea. Especially when you're sure it's never going to go anywhere but the bedroom.

That didn't mean I'd stopped wanting him. No, far from it. Every time he touched me, my skin burned. I took a step to the side, putting distance between us. "Excuse me," I said, cutting in. "I need to talk to Dax for a second if you don't mind."

The young shifter who'd been talking jerked his head in

my direction and his mouth fell open as he stared at me. His eyes widened then he shook his head, his too-long locks falling into his face. He brushed his hair back and asked, "You're Phoebe?"

"The one and only. And you're…?"

"Leo." He blinked and stood there, mute, until his blond friend nudged him in the gut with his elbow. Leo cast the other young shifter a glare, but when he turned back to me, he was all smiles and googly eyes. "Sorry. This is my friend Dali. We're… ah, friends of Dax."

My lips twitched with amusement. "I can see that. It's nice to meet you both. Is this your first time attending one of Allcot's galas?"

They both nodded. Then Leo leaned in. "It's a little strange for shifters to be at a vamp-sponsored party, isn't it?"

"Yes, but it's all part of the plan to end the tensions in the city," I said. Vampire and shifter relations in the city had deteriorated rapidly after Allcot had been apprehended by a rogue group of shifters a few months ago. Since then, both shifters and vampires from all over the city had started going missing and both groups were blaming each other. It was only after Dax had stepped in to facilitate a truce that they somehow managed to come together for Willow's cause. And because vamps and shifters alike had a vested interest in a neutral supernatural hospital, they'd both been invited.

The only question was could they make it through the evening without any bloodshed?

"Ladies and gentleman," the emcee started, but my attention was diverted when Dax stiffened beside me.

"What is it?" I asked him, scanning the crowd.

"Leo. He—"

Both of our phones beeped simultaneously, indicating

we'd been called to track down a vampire. "Shit," I muttered when I glanced at the screen and read the text. There was a description of the mark. *Approximate age thirty years old, one hundred sixty pounds, six foot tall, bright red hair. Last seen on Bourbon Street entering Peaches.* I rolled my eyes. "It figures it'd be a strip club."

Dax let out a barely audible growl of frustration, his gaze still locked on Leo. The young shifter was surrounded by five vampires and the conversation didn't look friendly. Worse, Leo wasn't keeping his cool. He had a snarl painted on his face and his muscles were rippling as if he was getting ready to shift right there in the ballroom. Dax turned to me. "I have to deal with that now before this gets any worse. Can you go ahead and I'll meet you down on Bourbon?"

I waved a hand. "Don't worry about it. I've got this one. You just keep them from turning this into an all-out vamp-shifter brawl."

"You're sure?" he asked.

"I better be, because it looks like another one of your shifters is getting ready to join the fray."

"Shit." Without hesitation, Dax took off and jumped right into the middle of the circle. The vamps immediately backed up, but they didn't disperse, and Leo wasn't anywhere near calm. Still, if anyone could defuse the situation, it was Dax.

My phone buzzed again. I typed back a response, letting our handler know I was on my way. Then I turned on my heel and headed out to do what I did best.

Chapter Two

---

*A*n ominous rumble of thunder crackled overhead as a gust of wind chilled me to the bone. I glanced up at the angry night sky and scowled. My silver dress wasn't going to fare well in a thunderstorm. Neither were my leather ankle boots. I cursed myself for forgetting to stock the car with a fresh change of clothes. I usually did, but I'd used my jeans and T-shirt during my last tracking mission and forgotten to replace them.

I clutched the lightweight overcoat around my body and prayed the weather held out at least long enough for me to make it to Peaches. Two more blocks to go. More thunder rumbled. I reached in my pocket and clasped my hand around my sun agate. The smooth, cool surface centered me. The agate had served me well over the past few years. One flash had the power to knock a vamp on his ass. With any luck, this run would be over within minutes, especially if my mark wasn't expecting me.

A gust of wind whistled through the air and blew up my

skirt, and I shivered. "Fuck." I quickened my pace, but it was no use. The dark, angry skies opened up and unleashed a massive torrent of rain.

Tourists scattered into bars, restaurants, and hotels, their shrieks of alarm muffled by the storm. I kept on, the rain drenching me in mere seconds. With the tourists out of the way, it took no time at all to reach the entrance of Peaches.

I slipped through the door and came to a dead stop when one of the strippers let out a gasp.

"Oh, honey. Bless your heart, you look like a drowned rat."

I cut my gaze to the woman wearing a strapless satin slip that barely covered her crotch. Her dark hair was piled high on her head and secured with a number two pencil, and she was wearing plastic-rimmed black glasses.

"Here, sweetheart." A man about twice my height and three times my weight wrapped a thick towel around my shoulders. "We were starting to wonder if you were going to make it at all. Dry off and go find something sexy to slip into. You're on in ten minutes. Minnie, show Carol to the dressing room."

What? I opened my mouth to protest but suddenly closed it. They thought I was a stripper. I almost laughed out loud. But getting into the back of the house would certainly help me with the element of surprise when tracking my vamp. I tightened the towel around my body and smiled up at him. "Thanks."

"You're welcome. Good luck out there." He scanned my body, his gaze lingering on my chest. I glanced down to see my jacket gaping open and one breast nearly falling out of the dress. At least I looked the part.

Minnie gave me a flat stare then jerked her head toward a door that read *Employees Only*. "This way, new girl."

I fell into step beside her.

She held the door open for me and followed me into the dank hallway. Once we were in the small dressing room, she took a good look at me and shook her head. "Didn't you bring anything to change into?"

"Um, no. I was planning on wearing this." I opened my coat and flashed her my short silver dress.

She rolled her eyes. "Newbies." Waving at a rack of barely there lingerie, she added, "Pick something from these loaners, but make sure you put it back when you're done. And those shoes… They have to go." She crossed the room and opened a cabinet. "Size?"

"Six."

She rummaged around while I rifled through the shoddy outfits on the rack. There was no flipping way I was borrowing anything from the other girls. All I had to do was wait for Minnie to leave and I'd slip out to the edge of the stage and spy my vamp.

"Here." She spun around and handed me a set of clear plastic shoes. "Why aren't you dressed yet?" Minnie stalked over to the rack and yanked out a sequined tube dress. "Here. This is close to what you were going to wear."

I held it up to my torso and wondered how it was going to cover my tits and my crotch at the same time.

Minnie tugged my coat off and had the zipper down on my dress before I even registered what was happening. "Nice blade," she said, sounding impressed. "You comfortable enough to use that if someone rolls up on you?"

I rewarded her with an audacious grin. "Wouldn't carry it if I wasn't."

Respect flashed in her knowing gaze as she nodded. "Good for you." Then she eyed my ass with an appraising look. "You'll want to keep an eye on that G-string. You wouldn't want it to walk away on its own. "

"Walk away? You mean the patrons might swipe it?" I shuddered, thinking about some random dude pressing his face against the scrap of fabric.

"Them or one of the other girls. The expensive stuff seems to always get swiped."

"Um, gross." If I'd thought some dude sniffing my used panties was disgusting, the idea that some other woman would wear my ass-crack floss made me want to gag.

"You said it, sister. Now put that thing on and go shake your ass." She stepped back and crossed her arms over her chest as she waited for me.

I shimmied into the tube dress and stepped into the clear, six-inch platform shoes.

Minnie let out a sigh and pounced on me, doing something to quickly tame my wet hair. She stepped back and eyed me critically. "Not exactly ready for a centerfold shot, but you'll do for a round on the stage." Her eyes narrowed in on the blade still strapped to my thigh that the tube dress was doing nothing to hide. "Gonna keep that thing on?"

"Yes," I said without hesitation even as I eyed my coat, my fingers itching for my sun agate.

"Just be sure you don't stab yourself while sliding down that pole." She grabbed my hand and started tugging me toward the door. "Time to get on stage."

"Wait." I twisted out of her grip and ran back to my coat. Once I had the agate in my hand, I stuffed it down my bra, knowing full well there was no way I'd be exposing myself no matter what Minnie and the club bouncer thought. All I needed was the element of surprise and that vamp wouldn't know what hit him.

"Come on. Hurry. They're waiting." Minnie pushed me out the door, and I found myself in a small alcove, barely hidden by the stage's curtain. In fact, a few of the patrons on the far side had already seen me and one of them stuck two fingers into his mouth and produced an ear-splitting whistle. What the hell had I been thinking? This was in no way an advantage to scouting out the vampire. In fact, I was basically trapped. I either strode out onto the stage where I'd be on full display—in more ways than one—or I made a small scene and ran back into the dressing room.

Better to play the part. If the vampire knew a tracker was after him, he'd never believe I'd show up as a stripper. Taking a deep breath, I strutted out on the stage, swaying my hips to "Candy Shop" by 50 Cent, grateful the song wasn't a faster rock number. It was much easier to strut around the stage making jerky pelvic motions than it would've been if I'd been expected to actually, you know, dance. I took my time scanning the club. Plush seats lined the stage and the walls while linen-covered tables filled in the center. There were expensive-looking chandeliers hanging from the ceiling, and the floors were lined with wall-to-wall carpet. It was a far cry from the sticky floors and plastic chairs one would find in most of Bourbon Street's strip clubs.

I grabbed the pole with one hand and whipped myself around, pausing for just a moment in time with the music. The action allowed me to study a tall man in the back of the club. He was in the shadows, making it difficult to make out his hair color, but he was distinct from everyone else, his movements more graceful and his presence commanding.

There was no doubt in my mind he was my mark. And he kept eyeing the front door as if he was waiting for someone.

Was he waiting for his next meal to walk in, or had someone tipped him off I was coming for him? The song continued on and I made ridiculous jerking motions, some of which seemed to resonate with at least a couple of people in the front row because dollar bills had been laid down on the stage. I knew that meant I should give them some individual attention, but that wasn't happening. I wasn't getting paid enough for this shit.

I did, however, decide they deserved a little more pole action before the song ended, and I put my considerable athletic skills to the test as I leaped forward and used only my arm strength to climb to three-quarters of the way to the top. Then I wrapped my knees around the pole and let go, bending backward so that my head was pointed straight down to the floor. I was just about to let myself slide down, using only my legs to stop me, when my goddamned sun agate fell right out of my bra and bounced across the stage, its light shining like a fucking beacon.

There was a loud gasp as all the supernaturals in the room recognized the artificial sunlight. Half a dozen newbie vamps screamed and ran for the exit. But not the vamp I'd identified at the back of the club. No, he was staring at me curiously, then he stepped forward into the light, revealing his bright red hair, a small, satisfied smile on his full red lips.

"Shit!" This was some sort of a setup. There was no doubt in my mind. I grabbed the pole with both hands and let myself quickly slide to the stage. My eyes stayed locked on the vampire as I hurried over to grab my agate. But as soon as I reached for it, one of the patrons grabbed it and snarled at me.

Shifter. A mean one too, judging by the snarl on his face. He held it up, showing it to me. The sunlight had faded, but the agate still glowed. "Look what I found. Since you didn't show us those sweet tits of yours, I think I'll just keep this little gem."

"Keep?" I scoffed, my hands digging into my hips. "I don't think so, wolf. Hand it over, or I'll kick you in the balls so hard you'll be choking on them."

"Feisty." He leered, his lips turning into a predatory smile. "I like the ones who fight back."

"Then you're gonna love the shit out of me." I jumped off the stage and kicked out, hitting him right in the chest with my clear plastic stripper shoe.

He fell backward, and both of us hit the floor, knocking tables and chairs over. The collision bothered neither of us, and in seconds we both rolled and landed back on our feet.

"Ready to hand it over, or do you want me to make good on my promise?" I asked.

His eyes narrowed and he made a show of stuffing the agate into his front pocket.

"Wrong move." I charged him, ducked a blow and went for his knee, just a quick jab. Then when he was off-balance, I went in for the kill—one brutal blow to the groin. He fell over sideways with a guttural groan. I pounced, stuffed my hand in his pocket, and retrieved my agate. "Try not to throw up," I whispered into his ear. "You wouldn't want to be stuck with a cleaning bill."

I stood up, scanned the awed faces, and winced. So much for undercover stealth. My eyes met the redheaded vamp's. An amused expression flashed over his face for just a moment before he winked and vanished out a side door.

"Son of a…" I darted back onto the stage and bolted for

the door back into the dressing room. Hunting a vampire was one thing, but doing it in stripper gear was entirely another. I hurried over to where I'd left my clothes and let out a curse. My dress and jacket were gone, but my phone was resting in the sole of my ankle boots. I stuffed my feet into them, grabbed the phone, and without further thought, I took off after the vamp, still wearing my barely there turquoise tube dress.

For once, Bourbon Street was mostly deserted. Even intoxicated party-types weren't much for braving the rain. Luckily for me, the storm had died down to a drizzle. Still, I was barely dressed and freezing my ass off. No matter. I had a vampire to catch.

I stopped just outside the club, tightened my grip on the agate, and pictured the redheaded vamp in my mind. Warmth spread from the agate, and a tiny buzz tickled my palm. He was definitely still around, closer than he should've been, considering I'd been made. Any other vamp would've hightailed it out of the neighborhood. Or at least one who knew what was good for him.

This one didn't. He was close. I moved to the right, and the vibration in the agate intensified. A pleased smile claimed my lips. After Willow had retired, I'd been determined to figure out some sort of vampire-detection tool. And thanks to a drop of Willow's blood and one of my spells, we'd managed to do just that. Because of her and that spell, I'd become the most successful vampire tracker in New Orleans.

My boots clamored on the sidewalk as I moved at a steady clip, making no move to indicate I knew exactly where the vampire was hiding—across the street, one building over, on the second story. I kept moving, certain he was watching me. I had two choices: one, stride right into the building, giving up any element of surprise, or two, circle the block and see if he followed me. If not, I'd find a way up onto the roof and go from there. I was just about to opt for door number two when the damned vampire strode right out onto the balcony and whistled.

He actually whistled, intending to get my attention.

What the hell was this? Some elaborate game of cat and mouse? Arrogant prick. Not one to back down, I stopped dead in my tracks and stared up at him. "You ready to get your ass kicked?"

"I can hardly wait." He flashed his fangs and jumped up, climbing to the next level and then onto the roof. He took off running, hopping from roof to roof, but his movements were slow. Much slower than a normal vampire's. He was taunting me.

And really pissing me off. Whatever game he was playing, I wasn't at all interested. The tube dress was doing nothing to keep me warm, and my stomach was starting to rumble. I'd had enough. Moving to the middle of the street, I raised my arms in the air and shouted, "Come get me vampire. I'm waiting for you."

He stopped, laughed, and stepped off the roof, his body floating effortlessly to the ground. His eyes flashed a brilliant green as he moved toward me.

Holy fuck. What he really that stupid? Or... son of a bitch. I held the agate straight out in front of me and cried, "*Siste!*"

Brilliant white light lit up the street and slammed into the vampire's chest. He stumbled back, paused for just a moment, and then resumed moving forward.

"Balls," I muttered, not at all surprised he'd been mostly unaffected by my sun agate. Normally a blast like that would put a vamp out for hours, giving me enough time to call in the cleaners from the Void. But his obvious self-confidence combined with the strange cat and mouse game he was playing meant he wasn't afraid of me. And there was only one other vampire in New Orleans who didn't give me a wide berth at all times—Eadric Allcot. If this vampire was as powerful as the leader of Cryrique, I had my work cut out for me.

"Phoebe Kilsen," he said. "It sure is good to see you out here tonight."

"Oh? And why's that?" I asked, judging the distance between us, surprised that Bourbon Street was suddenly deserted. Or maybe I shouldn't have been, considering a witch and vampire were facing off, both of us displaying powerful supernatural forces. If I could just get close enough I had confidence my paralyzing spell had enough oomph to at least give me a chance to neutralize his ass.

He glanced down at his watch. And when he looked back up at me, his expression was sinister. "It means that pretty soon that phone clutched in your hand is going to ring, and then your world is going to crumble."

What the hell was he talking about? I didn't have much of anything to lose. My job was just a means to an end. That left the people in my life. Dax could take care of himself, which meant— I let out a sharp breath and said, "Tal and Willow."

Satisfaction flashed in his eyes. Suddenly I couldn't breathe. *Tal and Willow.* This piece of shit had something planned for the only two people I loved. An ache formed in my gut and quickly morphed into pure rage as my phone rang, the sound eerie in the quiet night.

The vampire's throaty laugh made something snap inside me, and instead of reaching for the phone, I lunged for him.

My fingers barely scraped his cold skin before he leaped out of my grasp, landing a good ten feet away.

Knowing it wouldn't incapacitate him, I flung my hand out again and aimed the agate at him. This time I felt the word deep in my gut and repeated, "*Siste!*"

The light blasted him, bringing him to his knees. And when he hit the asphalt, I was already on him, both hands wrapped around his throat. Pure hatred radiated from his eyes as he stared up at me, motionless.

"Never mess with a Void witch or the people she loves," I snarled and squeezed harder, not that it would do any good. He was a vampire for Christ's sake. It wasn't like he needed to breathe, and crushing his windpipe was completely useless. But it made me feel better to inflict any bit of pain on the piece-of-shit vamp.

"You can't kill me," he ground out, his words barely audible.

"Maybe, maybe not, but I sure as hell can make you suffer." Then in one swift movement, I grabbed the dagger from my thigh and stabbed him right in the gut. He went limp and fell over, completely paralyzed.

I scrambled off him and reached for my phone. It had stopped ringing, but a text had popped up. It was from Dax indicating to call him ASAP. I hit his number and the second he answered I said, "It's Tal and Wil. They're missing, aren't they?"

His voice was tired and weary when he forced out "Yes."

Chapter Three

*T*he wait for the cleaners to arrive was pure torture. The moment I ended the call with Dax, I placed a call to the Void, requesting backup. They needed to apprehend the vamp, and since my dagger and I were the only things preventing his rising from the dead, I couldn't leave until they arrived.

Pacing, I worried my bottom lip. Who could've taken Tal and Willow and why? The why was pretty simple. Willow had a special power that could turn vampires into daywalkers. Every vampire hive in existence wanted that ability. Allcot had been doing his best to keep her secret under wraps since Willow had accidentally discovered her ability by turning one of his vamps. But secrets like that had a way of spreading like wildfire.

He'd made it known Willow Rhoswen belonged to him and that anyone who came after her or her family would suffer a fate worse than death. I wasn't quite sure what he meant by that, but knowing Allcot, it involved some sort of heinous torture.

If Willow hadn't been so vulnerable to the vampire community, she'd have never accepted his offer of protection. But when choices are limited, everyone does what they have to in order to survive. So far no hive had been willing to test Allcot's warnings. None until now.

It was bad enough the Cryrique vamps were on the verge of war with the shifters. Now there was a rival vampire hive blatantly defying Allcot's orders. If Allcot managed to find them, it was going to be a goddamned bloodbath. Hell, it'd be a bloodbath if I found them.

A few brave tourists made their way into the street. They were hesitant as they craned their necks, trying to see if it was safe to gawk at the staked vampire. A tall blonde met my eyes, and I honestly had no idea what she saw there, but whatever it was, it seemed to give her courage. She stepped forward, her head bowed. Then she sank to her knees beside the vampire and started to pray for his soul.

"Oh, for fuck's sake," I muttered, thoroughly annoyed. "What makes you think he has a soul?"

"Everyone does," she said in a matter-of-fact tone. "Even if it's hidden."

"This one doesn't," I snarled and grabbed her arm, yanking her up. "Don't you understand? He's a vampire. And if my spell stops working and he wakes up, what do you think is going to happen when he sees your creamy neck right there just waiting for the taking?"

She stiffened, her shoulders rigid and her lips tight.

"He's going to sink his teeth right into you. If you're lucky, you'll survive. If you're not... Well, these few moments you have right now, getting your chance to see a vampire up close and personal, are likely to be your last. Vamps who wake up from a magically induced coma usually are starving."

"Is that... um, likely?" she stammered. "Waking up before you release the spell?"

I shook my head. "No. But it can and does happen, especially if they're powerful. And this one is, so get the hell out of here, all right?"

Her hand flew to the hollow at her throat, and she began to slowly move backward. She kept her eyes trained on the redheaded vamp, fear in her eyes.

Okay, so I was being a tiny bit melodramatic. He was highly unlikely to wake up before I removed my dagger. But the last thing I needed was a circle of tourists gaping at the vamp. They could get their fill of actual vampires at any number of clubs around the city if they were brave enough to frequent them.

After Hurricane Katrina blew through over a decade ago, parts of the city were taken over and revitalized by vampires. Mid-City was full of them as well as much of Frenchmen Street. In my opinion, the vampire infusion had been as much a blessing as a curse. They had helped restore New Orleans when the rest of the country seemed to forget about the town, but they'd also brought danger, death, and deception. For those who never mixed with vampires, it was easy to pretend nothing was amiss. But when a vampire had someone in their sights? All bets were off. The vampires of New Orleans, and more specifically Eadric Allcot and his hive, could be ruthless, and they stopped at nothing until they got what they wanted.

And that's where I and my fellow vampire hunters came

in. It was our job to make sure they didn't get too far out of line.

"Kilsen. What do we have here?" Wallace Franks knelt down beside the vampire. "Looks like you had to pull out all the stops to bring him down."

I snorted. "You could say that."

The cleaner's gaze focused on me and he did a double take. "What the hell are you wearing?"

I glanced down at the turquoise tube dress. The drizzle had not been kind. The material had turned see-through, and if it hadn't been for my bra and panties, I'd be a prime candidate for indecent exposure. "Fuck me," I muttered. "Don't ask. Long story."

Franks shrugged out of his shirt and handed it to me. "Here."

I took the black button-down and wrapped it around myself, grateful there was at least one chivalrous man—or shifter to be exact—left in this town. "Thanks."

"No problem. Want to give me the highlights on this one?"

"Quickly. I've got another case—" My voice broke on the word *case*. Willow and Tal weren't just a case. They were family. "Um, an emergency actually."

His expression turned to one that looked an awful lot like pity, and I knew he'd already heard about the fae couple. "Understood."

"He's wanted for feeding off humans. One went missing yesterday. I tried to neutralize him with my agate, but he's too strong. It took my dagger to paralyze him. I'm positive if I take it out, he'll wake right back up."

"Got it." He pulled a large needle out of his bag and jabbed it into the vamp's neck.

I didn't have to ask what he was doing. The substance he was injecting into the vampire was highly controlled by the Arcane. It could knock a vampire out for hours before he regained consciousness. It was a fantastic drug as it didn't leave any permanent damage and vamps were alert fairly quickly after the affects wore off.

However, it was only ever used when and if a vamp had already been neutralized. If the vampire got it away from a tracker and used it on them, it was instant death. Too dangerous. So dangerous, in fact, the Arcane had banned it twice. But a few months ago, a vampire I'd stunned had awoken in the back of the van before they'd reached the Void offices and the vampire had gone mad, killing the two cleaners and driving the van off the Crescent City Connection bridge. After that incident, it had become a mandatory procedure to pump any vampire full of the toxin before transporting him or her to the holding cells.

I wrapped my hand around the handle of my dagger as Franks shoved his giant needle back into his bag of tricks. "Ready?"

"Ready."

Tightening my hold on the handle, I yanked the blade out of the vampire. His hand shot straight up and grabbed Franks by the neck. The cleaner let out a strangled gasp and tried to jerk back, but it was no use. The vampire's hold was too strong.

Without a second thought, I slammed the blade back into the vampire. He froze, his hand still clutching Franks's neck. I moved around them and started to pry the vamp's fingers off Franks. But suddenly the vamp started to vibrate, and before I could process what was happening, he yanked the blade out of his abdomen and slammed it into my thigh.

I let out a cry of pain and rolled. Fire burned up my leg and quickly headed for my chest. There were only seconds to spare. If the magic touched my heart, I'd be dead. My fingers wrapped around the cold hilt and I yanked while simultaneously zeroing in on the curse filling my veins. My magic flared to life and I mentally directed it to concentrate around the curse, to expel it through the blood already gushing from my wound.

Sweat poured down my face and my vision blurred, but I knew my magic was working. I could still feel the burn of the curse, and it was indeed flowing out of me. My wound was on fire, filling every sense that I had. I clutched my thigh and waited it out. Finally, when the burning stopped and my head swam from too much blood loss, I tore Franks's shirt off and staunched the wound.

"Phoebe!"

Dax's voice entered my consciousness and I raised my head, trying to blink away the blurriness clouding my vision. "Dax?"

"Jesus. What happened?" Even though his voice was rough and clouded with worry, I instantly calmed. Dax's presence comforted me, gave me something to focus on other than the fact that there was a gaping wound in my thigh and I'd probably lost enough blood that I'd need a transfusion.

"Powerful vampire. Too fucking powerful." I turned my head, scanning the area, already knowing the bastard was gone. He'd gotten away, and there was nothing I could've done about it.

"Shit!" Dax shifted away from me and he said, "Franks! Franks! Son of a bitch!"

I followed the sound of his voice and the blurry outline of Wallace Franks came into view. He wasn't moving.

Resignation settled over me and I whispered, "He's gone, isn't he?"

"Broken neck."

My eyes stung with angry tears as I dragged myself over to the cleaner I'd known for the past five years. He'd been one of the best. I placed my hand on his chest right over his heart, knowing I wouldn't feel anything, but praying Dax was wrong and that life still beat inside him.

Nothing. As Dax called in the incident, I laid my head on his chest and whispered, "Goodbye."

Chapter Four

"*T*ake me back to the gala," I said from the passenger seat of Dax's beat-up Trooper. Not long after he'd called in Franks's death, two more cleaners had shown up, taken my statement, then hauled Franks away. Without a word, Dax had picked me up and stuffed me into his Trooper.

"Are you insane? We need to get you to a healer ASAP." He barely slowed as he cranked the wheel and made a right turn, heading back toward Uptown.

Talisen's smiling face swam behind my closed eyelids. "But Tal and Willow—"

"Phoebe—"

"They are *family*," I bit out. "I can't keep fucking around, knowing someone has them. Some vampire hive that is likely one of Allcot's enemies. Who knows what they'll do to them?"

"You know as well as I do they aren't going to hurt Willow. If they took her, they did it for her abilities," he said, his voice clear and assured as he slipped into tracker mode. "They'll want to keep her strong so she can turn as many of their vamps as possible."

"But they won't hesitate to hurt Tal. Especially if they're trying to make her do something she doesn't want to do. I have to get back there and cast a tracing spell."

He glanced over at me, his eyes narrowed. "You really think you have the strength to do a tracing spell?"

"Yes," I said without hesitation, but it was a lie. My hands had started to shake, and I was so cold my feet had gone numb.

He grunted and continued driving.

"I can't…" I swallowed the ache at the back of my throat.

"Can't what?" He stepped on the gas, flying down the road, his impatience finally showing.

"It was a fucking setup, Dax. The vampire who did this to me? He baited me, toyed with me just long enough to snatch them. This was planned."

He jerked his head, staring at me. "Planned? But how? There were three dozen Cryrique vampires at the gala. Not to mention an entire pack of shifters. There is no way a rogue hive could've taken them unless—"

"Allcot was in on it," I finished for him, finally making the connection. Of course he was. He'd sent some unknown vamp to keep me occupied, to taunt me and throw me off the trail. Did he really think I was that stupid? That I wouldn't see right through his shitty plan? If I hadn't been so angry about Willow and Tal's disappearance, I'd have been insulted.

"There's no other way. No one gets past Allcot's goons without his say-so."

"I'll kill the bastard," I ground out.

"Not before the healer gets you put back together," Dax said.

I opened my mouth to protest, to demand he turn around and head back downtown, but no sound came out. Instead, my world began to spin, and suddenly everything went dark.

THE LOW MURMUR of voices coaxed me from my dark cocoon of slumber. My limbs were heavy, as if they were weighted down, and my lids didn't seem to want to open. I tried to move my lips, to speak, to turn my head, to do anything to pull myself from a shadow world where I hovered in the in-between.

"It's not the blood loss that's the problem," a woman with a silky voice said. "We've already hooked up the transfusion."

"What do you mean by *problem*?" Dax asked.

"She can't fully recover until we purge the dark magic that was used on her. See this?"

"Yeah?"

"These dark edges indicate a curse. A powerful one, and it's preventing the stitching spell from doing its job. She'll have to stay until we can figure out what to do."

"She's not going to like that one bit," Dax said.

If I could've smiled, I would've. My partner knew me all too well.

"It can't be helped."

Ice-cold hands touched my thigh, and my voice came back as I let out a displeased groan.

"Phoebe?" Dax's breath tickled my cheek, and my eyes finally flew open.

Pure fear stared back at me through his gaze and I

suddenly pushed myself up. "What's wrong? What happened? Is it Wil? Tal? Tell me they're all right."

Dax's full lips curved into a pleased smile. "Welcome back, Phoebs."

I scowled at him. "Dax! Wil, Tal?"

He shook his head. "No news yet."

"They why did you look like someone had…" I trailed off, remembering that we'd just lost Franks. And while that had hit both Dax and me pretty hard, it wasn't the first time we'd lost an agent of the Void, and it wouldn't be the last. Whatever had scared him was something different. "Uh, I mean, why were you looking at me like that?"

He shook his head slightly. "It might be because for a moment there I thought you'd checked out on me. For the record, Kilsen, you're not allowed to pass out on me ever again. Got it?"

Jesus. The wound must be bad, because in all my years of hunting vampires and suffering concussions, bite wounds, and even broken bones, I'd never once passed out. Phoebe Kilsen, badass vampire hunter, *did not* faint. Ever. I cleared my throat. "That's a promise I'll gladly make."

"Ms. Kilsen," the silky-voiced woman said. "Welcome back."

I blinked up at her. She had lush auburn hair that was pulled back into a long ponytail, wide-set blue eyes, and flawless porcelain skin. She was also wearing a silver-gray lab coat with her name embroidered on the left side. Healer Imogen.

"Hello," I said, raising my eyebrows. "Are you new in town? I haven't seen you here before."

Her lips morphed into a radiant smile. "Just arrived last week. I have to say, New Orleans has had some of the most interesting cases I've ever had the opportunity to work on. This week has been incredible. But then you walked in."

"Um, and now it's not… incredible, I mean?"

"Oh, it is. Definitely," she gushed. "But that wound, and the way you forced the curse out of your body. I've never seen a witch do that before. Not on herself. Are you a healer too?"

I snorted out a chuckle. "No, just stubborn."

"Thank the gods you are," she said as she flipped the heavy blanket covering me off my leg. "If you weren't, we'd have lost you."

A sick ache suddenly materialized in my stomach. I pressed a hand to my stomach and said, "I didn't have much of a choice."

"I wish all my patients were as stubborn as you. Now, what can you tell me about this curse?"

"Nothing."

The left side of Dax's lips twitched. I knew instinctively they'd already had this conversation. Well, if she thought she was getting details on my family curse, she'd lost her mind.

"You don't know anything about it?" she said, her tone incredulous.

"No, I do," I said, shifting position and swinging my legs over the edge of the bed. "I just can't tell you anything about it. Family secret."

"Ms. Kilsen, if we're going to heal your wound, I'm going to need to know something about the curse. I need a starting point."

"No, you don't," I said, inspecting my thigh. I didn't exactly remember what it looked like after the vampire had stabbed me. My recollection was hazy. But considering I'd been running out of strength and blood when I'd forced the magic out of my system, the fact that there was only a thin outline of the curse still remaining meant I'd done a damn fine job. The area wasn't even red or swollen.

"The curse will spread," she insisted, sounding frantic.

I just shook my head and placed my palm over the wound. Closing my eyes, I pictured the wound in my mind and whispered, "*Sano.*" Magic concentrated in my thigh, tingling with brilliant energy. The wound stung, causing me to suck in a sharp breath, and then it began to burn. The fiery-hot pain was so intense it felt as if actual flames were licking over my skin. But underneath it all was my prickly magic, doing the job I'd asked it to do.

"Damn, Phoebe," Dax said, awe in his tone.

I opened my eyes, focusing on him. He was staring down at my leg, his eyebrows raised and an expression of wonder on his face.

"I've never seen anything like that before," Imogen said.

I followed their gazes to my thigh and let out a small gasp of surprise. My hand was glowing silver, but instead of still covering the wound, it was hovering over it, a thick fog of black smoke clinging to my palm. I raised my hand, turned it over, and said, "Release."

The dark smoke dissipated into the air and hovered as if suspended. I leaned forward, gently blowing. The smoke suddenly vanished into thin air as if it had never existed. And my thigh? All that was left of the wound was a small pink scar.

A pleased smile claimed my lips as I turned my attention to the healer. "I think I'll be fine now."

"How…?" She shook her head. "That was unreal. You must have healer magic. There's no other explanation. I just can't—"

I held a hand up. "It's because I created the curse. Or

rather my great-grandmother did, and it's controlled by blood," I explained and hopped off the bed. Gooseflesh broke out over my bare skin and I glanced down, realizing I was only wearing my bra and panties. It was a damned good thing Dax had already seen me naked. Otherwise, that moment would've been really awkward. "Now, where's my dress?"

Dax held up the turquoise tube dress.

I grimaced. "Damn. I forgot about that."

"Care to explain what happened to your gala dress?" he asked.

"Later. Right now all I'm interested in is getting out of here." I tugged the tube dress over my head. "Shoes?"

Dax pointed to the corner of the room. The boots were on the floor while my dagger and phone were sitting in the seat of a metal folding chair.

I strode over, slipped them on, and grabbed my belongings. "Thanks, Imogen," I said to the healer. "Whatever you did gave me my strength back, enough to eradicate the rest of the curse. I owe you one."

She shook her head. "No you don't. I was just doing my job."

"Maybe," I said, staring her in the eye. "But no one knows better than I do how powerful that curse is. I have no doubt that in the wrong hands, I might've never woken up."

Dax muttered a curse.

Imogen grabbed my free hand. "I don't like that you're leaving so soon, but I understand the urgency of your case. Please just promise me that if you have any dizziness, unexplained fatigue, or any other unusual symptoms that you'll come back in."

Her hands were warm around mine, soothing even. But

still her touch made me uneasy, and I frowned. That was strange. Talisen was the healer I usually saw after some vamp banged me up, and never once had his touch bothered me. I tugged my hand out of hers, the unease instantly vanishing, and nodded just so we didn't waste any more time there.

"Sure." I turned to Dax. "Let's go."

He led the way out of the exam room and into the quiet reception area. It was then I realized the healer's office was in an old Victorian. White sheers covered the bay windows while two velvet couches filled what used to be a parlor along with a large desk off to the side. I glanced at the clock on the wall. Five twenty-five a.m. No wonder the place was empty.

Dax held the door open for me and we slipped outside onto Saint Charles Avenue.

"Has Allcot gotten his hands on her yet?" I asked Dax. Eadric Allcot was notorious for getting his hooks in any witches with healing powers. The truly powerful ones he always tried to lure to Cryrique. And if he couldn't lure them, he used blackmail to get them to do his bidding.

It hadn't always been that way, but as his organization delved deeper into experimental drugs for the supernatural, the demand for quality healers rose significantly. And although I hadn't been able to prove anything yet, I was certain Allcot was breaking multiple laws when it came to testing those drugs. Unfortunately, the compromised healers were the ones running all his tests... mostly on unwilling participants, turning them into unwilling accomplices. If Allcot had gotten to her, there was no telling what she was doing behind closed doors at her clinic.

He shook his head. "No. She didn't even know who he was."

"You're sure about that?"

"I asked her and believed her when she said no. Then I warned her he'd likely try something." Dax paused beside the Trooper and eyed me. "Why?"

"Just a feeling. I'm not sure we can trust her."

He glanced back at the clinic, his eyes hooded. Then he grimaced and opened my door. "Get in. We have a couple of fae to find."

"It's about time," I said, a tiny twinge of relief rushing through me.

Dax ran around the Trooper and claimed the driver's seat. He cranked the key and as the engine rumbled, he said, "But first you need a change of clothes."

I stared down at the dirty, stained tube dress and nodded. I could kick a vampire's ass wearing nothing but a smile, but it would be a hell of a lot easier in my tracker uniform. Jeans, T-shirt, and boots. All of which held my arsenal of weapons that would make it easier to end whoever took Willow.

Chapter Five

*W*hen I opened the door to the Greek revival home I shared with Tal and Willow, I half expected to hear the murmur of my friends' voices upstairs. Instead, I walked through the door and was nearly knocked on my ass by a large gray wolf.

Link, Willow's wolf-shifting shih tzu, was in full-on agitated mode as he shoved his muzzle into my face and let out a low whine.

"Christ, you're a pathetic wolf," I said, gently patting the top of his head. He followed me into my bedroom and sat patiently as I pulled out fresh clothes and headed into my adjoining bathroom. The wolf followed me, his whine turning to a low growl.

"I know, Link. She's missing. But we can't do anything about it until I wash off this blood and climb into fresh clothes."

His amber eyes glowed with intelligence as he sat back down, waiting.

Link was at least one good thing in my favor. He'd been with Willow since he was a puppy and no one, not even Talisen, was more devoted to Willow than Link. If anyone could scent her out, it'd be him.

Ten minutes later, I was out of the shower, fully dressed, and armed. I had everything from my dagger to a couple of stakes to my magic-infused jewelry. I even had another blade tucked in my boot, though this one wasn't cursed. I ran upstairs with Link on my heels and found Dax in the kitchen, rummaging through the fridge.

Red marinara sauce had dried to the dirty dishes that were stacked beside the sink, an echo of the lasagna dinner the three of us had shared the previous night before we'd left for the gala.

I could still see Willow laughing as she slathered butter on yet another slice of french bread, insisting that just one more wouldn't hurt, and Tal rolling his eyes as the pair of us teased him about his pin-striped seersucker suit. He was a fae originally from northern California, not a Southern gentleman. Willow had flashed him one of her radiant smiles and assured him he'd be the most handsome man there. I, of course, had made a gagging sound because seriously, when you had to watch your two best friends fawn all over each other while you lusted after the shifter you couldn't have, sometimes your immaturity got the better of you.

My gaze shifted and landed on a brown paper bag. Some Like It Hot Chocolate was scrawled across the front in Willow's handwriting. Her concoction to promote fertilization was inside that bag. The one she'd mentioned at the gala. A small, strangled gasp escaped from my lips before I could stop it.

"Hey," Dax said, stepping in front of me and placing his large hands on my shoulders. "You okay?"

"They're supposed to be trying for a baby." My voice was low and shaky as I stared up at him, my vision suddenly blurred with emotion.

He let out a small sigh and pulled me to him, his strong arms holding me tight. "We're going to find them, Phoebs. I promise."

"I know," I snapped and jerked out of his embrace. I wasn't sure if I was more annoyed with him or myself. This weepy person, crying in the kitchen when I should've already been out the door tracking them both, wasn't me at all. And Dax of all people should've known that. I gritted my teeth and stared him right in the eye. "Don't comfort me."

"Why the hell not?" he shot back, annoyance flashing all over his handsome features. "Because I'm not your boyfriend? Not allowed to care about you? Well, I've got news for you, Kilsen. Just because you won't let me back into your bed doesn't mean I don't give a shit about you. Got it?"

I bit back a wince, knowing I deserved his ire. His only sin was that he'd cared too much. "That's not…" I ran a frustrated hand through my hair. "I don't fall apart. Ever."

"That's an understatement," he said, not breaking eye contact.

I gritted my teeth. "And I'm sure as hell not going to start now. Comfort is *not* what I need from you."

"So what the fuck am I supposed to do? Ignore the fact that you have tears in your eyes? Jesus, Phoebe. I'm not a fucking machine. I can't just turn off everything I'm feeling like—" He clamped his mouth closed and stared at the ceiling. "I'm not a robot."

"Of course you aren't," I shot back. Then I lowered my voice and added, "I'm not either, you know."

His unreadable gaze met mine as he waited for me to continue.

"I'm *not*," I said again. "But what I need from you right now is for you to kick my ass into gear. Falling apart is not an option. I'm stronger than that. I *have* to be stronger than that because right now we need to be focusing on finding Willow and Talisen. And the best thing you can do is to remind me of that, not be my savior."

"Savior?" he scoffed. "Impossible. You'd never allow that."

I sucked in a deep breath, willing myself to not scream at him. Then I let it out, and in a controlled, emotionless tone, I said, "I'm not doing this right now. If you want a fight, it'll have to wait." Then I grabbed one of Willow's energy bars off the counter, turned, and stalked out of the room, Link following at my heels.

"Shit," I heard Dax say. "Kilsen, wait."

I didn't slow down as I passed Willow and Tal's room. The door was open, revealing the enchanted tree that gave them strength in a city of concrete. My chest ached as I imagined them both locked away in some cell or building with no vegetation. Without nature, they'd both start to weaken, making them even more vulnerable. *Damn.*

Link turned his head, his golden eyes scanning the room. Then he shot down the stairs and paced in front of the door while he waited for me to catch up. "Don't worry. The two of us will find them, Link."

"The three of us will," Dax said, reaching past me to open the door.

I met his brilliant blue eyes and said, "Thank you."

"There's nothing to thank me for, Kilsen," he said. "Now get your ass out the door. We have a job to do."

My lips twitched in amusement. He'd heard me loud and clear and was giving me exactly what I needed. And damn if that wasn't sexy as hell. I slipped past him and headed for the Trooper. "You drive."

He cast a glance at my gunmetal-gray Charger, his eyebrows raised.

It was a good question. Given a choice, I'd usually take mine any day of the week. But today we had company. I waved a hand at Link. "He sheds."

Dax let out a deep laugh, shook his head, and climbed into the driver's seat of the Trooper, not bothering to open my door.

Finally, I thought. He was learning.

"SOMETHING TELLS me Bell Fountain Hotels won't be inviting the Cryrique back anytime soon," I said as Link and I stood in the middle of the ballroom, eyeing the utter destruction. The glass on the french doors that led to the balcony had been smashed to pieces. One had been completely ripped off the hinges. Food was smeared on the walls, flower petals swam in puddles of champagne, and there was blood spatter on the floor and one of the walls. "Tell me exactly what happened."

A muscle in Dax's jaw pulsed as I watched the anger boil inside him. He walked over to me and pointed to the balcony. "Remember when you left? I jumped into that altercation with Leo and those fucking vampires who were taunting him."

"Taunting?" I asked. "I thought it was just another vamp-shifter brawl. You know, when the two groups feed off the other's hostility until one finally snaps."

He gave me a derisive snort. "Yeah, I was expecting that too. But this was different, personal. The vampires, they knew stuff about Leo's family, bad shit that would fuck with anyone. And they knew about his record and the fact that he took the fall for a girl of his, who ran off with his mortal enemy the moment he was locked up."

"Ouch. That's fucked up."

"Tell me about it."

"And the vampires brought that shit up at the gala? Why?" I asked.

"I had no idea at the time." His expression turned murderous. "Now it makes sense."

A lightbulb popped on over my head. "A distraction?"

"Exactly. Right after you walked out of the gala, one of the vamps attacked Leo. You saw him. The kid was already on the verge of shifting."

"Let me guess. After that Leo couldn't control himself. And once he shifted, so did half the shifters in the ballroom."

"Half? Ha! Try three-quarters. Most of the shifters who showed up were young. Old guys like me usually don't want anything to do with Allcot or his lackeys."

Old guys. Dax was all of thirty years old. But I knew what he meant. The shifters at the gala had been young, early twenties like Leo and Dali, and most had been relatively new in town. "Okay, so I imagine all hell broke loose?"

"You could say that. I was busy keeping Leo from being torn apart. Meanwhile, the other shifters started attacking the vampires."

"Why?" I asked, jerking my head back in surprise.

"Instinct. Too young to control themselves. The next thing I knew, there was a full-on brawl. The minute I got Leo away from the vamps who'd been taunting him, I hauled him outside and sent him home. Then I ran back in to find Willow and Talisen. But…"

"They were already gone?" I filled in, my heart sinking.

He nodded then dropped his head, appearing defeated. When he glanced back up, sorrow and determination and guilt were shining back at me. "There is no doubt in my mind it was a setup. Everything from you being called away to the attack on Leo. The vampires did this. They took Willow and Talisen. I'm sure of it."

The night's events replayed in my mind. The redheaded vamp had been embarrassingly easy to find considering he'd done nothing to alter his appearance even after an alert had been issued for his description. I hadn't thought about it much at the time, but usually vampires weren't that stupid, not if they were trying to stay below the radar. But he definitely hadn't been. He'd waited for me to see him before he'd fled the strip club. He'd stayed nearby, making sure he'd be easy to track. Then he'd stalked right out into the street and all but challenged me to a duel.

I cursed. I'd thought we'd been set up. Now I was sure of it. "We've definitely been played."

Chapter Six

"Have you tracked Allcot down yet?" I asked Dax.

He shook his head. "While the healer was working on you, I got ahold of one of his vampires. He told me Talisen and Willow had been taken by one of the rival hives. He claimed he didn't know where Allcot was. Said the entire inner circle at Cryrique is in a frenzy."

"Do you believe him?" It was hard to imagine the Cryrique vampires being anything but in control. Allcot ran a tight ship. If what the contact said was true, it was possible Allcot wasn't responsible for Willow and Tal's disappearance, and if he wasn't, it sounded like they'd been just as surprised as we'd been.

"He sounded shaken, that's for sure. I don't think we'll know anything definite until we see Allcot."

I nodded. Allcot was a bastard. There was no doubt about that. But chances were high I'd know which way the wind was blowing after we spoke. Some people had a hard time seeing through his lies, but I didn't. His cockiness was always a dead giveaway. "Do we know for sure vampires took them? Not shifters?"

He crossed his arms over his chest and nodded. "I'd know it if the pack had their eye on Willow and Tal."

"Okay." I rubbed at my forehead, trying to figure out who else would've even had access to Willow and Tal at the gala. "The more I think about this, the more I'm inclined to believe this was all a big ploy by Allcot to finally lock Willow in his dungeon." At one point, Allcot had tried to force Willow to work for him, but over time they'd formed an uneasy truce. While she trusted him, I didn't. A vampire doesn't end up the head of one of the most powerful vampire organizations in the US without being a complete prick. And Eadric Allcot was definitely a prick. A self-serving, arrogant prick. And Willow had something extremely valuable to not only him but pretty much every other vampire in existence. If Allcot could control it, he'd be unstoppable.

"Fuck, you're right," he said, grabbing the back of his neck. "We just can't be sure of anything when the information comes from Allcot's goons."

"No, we can't. So that means we need to start from here." I turned to Link, who'd just returned from a scenting excursion around the ballroom. "Did you pick up her trail?"

Link lifted his head and ran toward the balcony. Dax and I followed him. The wolf stopped at the railing, turned around in a circle a few times, then sat down and sniffed at the bottom of one of the railing posts.

"They took her over this railing," I told Dax. "Come on. Let's go find out if there's a trail of her scent out on the street."

Dax and I started to move back into the ballroom, but

Link stayed exactly where he was, staring forlornly at the ground.

"Link, let's go," I ordered.

He didn't move and let out a sad whimper.

"Oh for the love of…" I bit back a curse and walked back over to the wolf. Crouching down, I placed both hands on the sides of his head. "Listen, buddy. I know you're missing her, but you need to pull it together."

He pawed at my foot.

I glanced down, scanning the area. Link put his nose to the ground and nudged something out of the shadows. I knelt and ran my hand lightly over the ground. My fingers closed over the cool stone, and I knew instantly what he'd found. "Good boy, Link," I said patting his head. "Very good boy."

"What is it?" Dax asked, squinting into the sunrise.

I held my hand out to him, showing him the crystal Willow usually wore around her neck. It was a protection crystal that Talisen had given her when they were teenagers. "She's going to be very pissed when she realizes this is missing."

Dax peered at my hand. "The clasp is broken on the chain. I think it's clear this is where the altercation happened." He glanced over the railing, down at the ground. "We're five stories up, which means the vampire who snagged them has to be powerful enough to fly."

"Willow can fly," I said.

"Sure. But unless she was attempting to escape, she wouldn't have gone over the side."

"No. But it is possible she fled over the railing. That doesn't explain Tal though." Male fae didn't have wings. And Willow's wouldn't have been able to support both of them. I shook my head. "Even if they did try, there's no doubt the

45

vamps eventually got them. Otherwise we'd have heard from them by now."

"Sounds right."

"Ready to go, Link?" I asked the wolf.

He moved to stand beside me.

"Good. Let's see if you can scent them." I took off for the door. And this time both Dax and Link followed.

Once we were out on the street, Link put his nose to the ground, furiously trying to sniff out his mistress, but it was no use. He circled the block twice, then sat at my feet and stared up at me, waiting for direction. I glanced at Dax. "Should we try the roof?"

He gave me a half shrug. "What good would that do? Even if Link can scent them, there won't be any kind of trail. Not if the vamp levitated right off the building."

I let out a frustrated sigh. He was right. It was impossible to track the ancient vampires the old-fashioned way. They just had too much power. It was time to try a tracing spell. I pulled out Willow's crystal and held it in my hand. Closing my eyes, I pictured first Willow, then Talisen. Magic tingled and burned hot through my veins. When I opened my eyes, my hand glowed with magic.

"Reveal," I whispered. The ball of light floated up from my hand, swelled, and formed a window allowing me to peek through the veil of the universe. A Willow-shaped shadow appeared and, slowly but surely, morphed into a picture of my friend. She was in a nondescript room void of any furniture, pacing back and forth. My only consolation was that she didn't appear to be hurt. Just a little rattled and clearly pissed off.

"Willow," I said, my voice loud and clear.

She stopped abruptly and frantically glanced around. "Phoebe? Are you out there?"

"I'm here, Wil. Where are you?"

"Phoebe?" she asked again.

"Come on, Wil, where are you," I whispered again, knowing she could feel my presence but couldn't see me or hear me.

"Dammit," she muttered and grabbed fistfuls of her hair in frustration. Growling, she straightened her shoulders, narrowed her eyes, and stared straight ahead, her gaze landing somewhere over my right shoulder. "Some rogue vampires got us, knocked us out, and hauled us away. Tal is here in another room. They let me see him a while ago. He's hurt, but I think once he gets his strength back, he'll survive. But here's the important part—I don't know where we are or who has us. So far they've only spoken to us over an intercom. It's somewhere high-tech. I saw Tal through a two-way mirror, but then it frosted over."

"Do you think Allcot's behind this?" I asked, even though I knew she couldn't hear me.

"I'd start at the Void building. Look in the records for something or someone called Asier. They specifically said they're looking forward to Asier's arrival." Her attention snapped to something across the room, and her eyes widened just before she launched herself at something. And just like that, my magical light vanished.

"Damn," I muttered.

"At least they're all right," Dax said, his angry tone belying his words of comfort.

"And we now know vampires took them," I said. "Probably not Allcot or else Willow would've said so."

"I agree. Not Allcot. At least not him personally or any of

his regular crew. She did give us a lead." Dax jerked his head toward the Trooper parked a few feet away. "Ready to get to work?"

I glanced at my watch. It was just before eight. Good. The Void research staff would be arriving shortly. "Ready. Let's see if we can find any intel on Red while we're searching the records for Asier."

~

SECURITY at the Void building had been beefed up recently, and when Dax and I walked in with Link, the guard I knew only as Arlo shook his head. "Nope. No shifters." He pointed at Link. "Whoever he is, he can't come through security."

"Dax is a shifter," I said reasonably. "You still let his shaggy ass in the building."

"Thanks, Phoebs," Dax said dryly.

"Ms. Kilsen, please don't try my patience," the older man said. "Mr. Marrok has security clearance. I've never seen this wolf before."

"Sure you have." I glanced down at Link. "Shift, boy."

The wolf stared up at me, his eyes narrowed.

"If they let you in here, it's just going to happen the minute you go through security anyway."

Link, who actually had been to this building more times than any of us could count, let out a huff. But a spark of light flashed over him, and a second later, a gold-and-white shih tzu was sitting at my feet, leaning into my leg.

I smiled at Arlo. "See? Hardly a security threat."

"Willow Rhoswen's pup?" he asked curiously.

"Yes. He's working with me for the time being." I pulled my dagger out of its holder and proceeded to unload the rest of my weapons and magic-infused jewelry into one of the baskets. Then Link and I walked through the scanner.

Arlo placed my basket into one of the lockers and handed me the key. If they went through the scanner, all my spells would be neutralized and rendered completely useless. Dax did the same, and together the three of us headed upstairs.

I was just about to round the corner to head into the research office when a young witch I recognized as the director's assistant ran up to me, clearly winded, and said, "Agent Kilsen, the director is waiting for you."

"She is?" I glanced back at Dax. "Did you get a directive?"

He shook his head.

"Director Halston wants you to report to her immediately," the young witch said, glancing over her shoulder. "It's urgent."

"Fuck me," I muttered. What else kind of shit had gone down last night? Whatever it was, the Void was just going to have to get some other agent, because I had two fae to find.

Dax immediately turned and started to make his way toward the director's office. Link stayed at my feet, waiting for my order. How come all shifters couldn't be as loyal as the shih tzu? I jerked my head, indicating we should follow Dax, and led Link into the west wing of the building.

"She's in there," the assistant said, her hand shaking as she pointed at Halston's office.

"Carla, right?" I asked, hoping I was remembering her name correctly.

"It's Marla." She gave me just a hint of a smile before she glanced nervously at the director's office again.

"Right. Marla. Um, is there something we should know before we walk in there?"

She nodded, but when she opened her mouth to speak, no sound came out. Her face turned ashen, and shaking her head, she ran back down the hall.

I met Dax's gaze and cursed the Void and their goddamned stupid security rules. There was something seriously wrong in Halston's office, and not only did I not have any weapons, but neither Dax or Link could shift into wolf form while in the building. The neutralizing scanner had seen to that. It'd be a few hours before they got their abilities back.

Walking with a calm that didn't actually exist, I moved to Marla's desk and pulled the top drawer open. I stifled a groan when all I found were extra pens and notebooks. "Come on, Marla," I said under my breath. She had to have something I could use as a weapon. A stapler, a letter opener—hell, a paperweight would be welcome at this point.

Dax, who'd obviously caught on to what I was doing, opened the drawers on the left while I took the right. Both of us quickly rummaged around. I scowled in annoyance at the drawer full of every snack under the sun. Pushing aside what had to be two dozen individually wrapped Kiss Me Chocolates, I shoved my hand into the back of the drawer. My fingers closed around a cool metal handle.

Yes! Jackpot!

I tugged the knife free and almost laughed at the bright pink handle. Good for Marla. I tucked it into the small of my back and turned to Dax. He held up a stun gun, indicating he'd been just as successful.

"How the hell do you think she got these past security?" I asked in a hushed tone.

"Halston. No doubt she gave them to her assistant just in case."

"Well, it's a good thing she did, even though Marla is probably off vomiting somewhere."

Dax stuffed the stun gun into his pocket and pressed his back to the wall on one side of Halston's door. I wrapped my hand around the hilt of the knife and did the same. Link, my new sidekick, stayed at my feet, obedient but on alert. Even in shih tzu form, his presence felt slightly ominous, and I started to seriously regret not taking one of his littermates… even if I would've had to sacrifice my entire shoe collection to a gnawing puppy.

Link and I hadn't gotten off to a great start. It's hard to love the creature who eats your favorite boots for dinner and your favorite red pumps for dessert. But now I was thinking it was a sacrifice worth making.

Dax slowly reached over to grab the doorknob. He looked up at me and I nodded, indicating I was ready. He nodded back and in the next second, he threw the door open and spun, the stun gun out as he scanned the room for danger. "Son of a bitch!" he yelled and flung himself into the room.

Without hesitation, I whipped the knife out and followed. The moment I stepped through the threshold, I froze, taking a moment to process the scene.

"Holy shit! Allcot, what the fuck are you doing?" I cried.

The blond vampire, who looked like he couldn't be a day over seventeen years old, had Halston hauled up against the wall and was holding her by the neck with one hand. Her face had turned almost purple, and she was clawing at his hand, indistinguishable sounds coming from her. He whipped his head around, his bloodshot eyes wild as he growled at me.

Dax shot forward, the stun gun sparking to life.

Allcot dropped Halston, just as I knew he would, and flew at Dax. The old vampire was so fast I barely saw him move.

But then he was on Dax, his hand wrapped around the shifter's wrist, and he squeezed, the bones crushing under his vise-like grip.

Dax roared and clocked Allcot in the temple with his free hand. More bones crunched, making me wince, but I wasn't sure if it was Allcot's face or Dax's fist. The vampire barely rocked back from Dax's powerful blow.

I rushed to Halston's side, dropping to my knees as Link ran back and forth barking, clearly frustrated he wasn't part of the action. "Director," I said, pressing two fingers to her neck right over her thready pulse. Good. She was still alive at least.

She let out a gargled choke. Then her eyes flew open and she sat straight up, her light blue wings fluttering in clear agitation. "What are you doing?" she rasped out as she pointed to Dax. "Are you just going to let Allcot kill him?"

"I was— Never mind." Grateful Allcot hadn't killed her, I shot to my feet. The old vampire had quickly overpowered Dax. The shifter was on his knees, and Allcot had grabbed a fistful of his hair, yanking his head back so far it was a wonder the vampire hadn't broken Dax's neck.

"Where. Did. They. Take. Her?" Allcot ground out. "You have one shot, shifter."

"That's exactly what we'd like to know," I said, my tone full of ice and fury. "Why the hell would Dax abduct Willow?"

"Willow?" Allcot let out a short humorless laugh. "Do you think I'd go through all the trouble to get to the director if I were here for Willow Rhoswen?"

"You have in the past," I said, crossing my arms over my chest, not believing him for a second. "I remember when you and your crew blew a hole in the wall to help her escape."

"That was business," Allcot said and yanked harder on Dax's hair. The shifter let out a high-pitched whine that I knew had to be involuntary. Dax would never willingly show weakness in front of Allcot. Allcot cast him a disgusted glance then added, "This is personal."

"Damn right it's personal. This is my best friend we're talking about. The fairy you swore you would protect from the other supernaturals in this city." Allcot and Willow were related. Sort of. His consort Pandora had family connections to Willow's nephew and the woman who would've been Willow's sister-in-law had her brother not perished in an untimely death. At Pandora's request, Allcot had agreed to keep them all safe. "Did you forget you made that promise to Pandora? What would she say about this?"

Allcot threw Dax against the wall. The shifter crashed into it, causing the plaster to shatter and fall around him. Link let out a howl and shot forward, running to Dax's side.

"Dax—" I started, but Allcot cut me off, backing me up until the backs of my legs hit Halston's desk.

Allcot's fangs extended as his ice-blue eyes pierced me. "This is not about Rhoswen, witch. I'm here for Pandora."

My mind whirled as I tried to parse exactly what he was telling me. "Pandora sent you?" That made no sense. Why would she think someone from the Void had taken Willow?

"She didn't send me, you fool!" Allcot roared as he picked me up by the shoulders and shook me as if I were a rag doll. I tightened my hand on the knife and tried to remain patient, waiting for my opening. "I'm here because— Oomph!"

Dax had come out of nowhere and smashed a metal chair over Allcot's head. Link was right beside him, barking his little shih tzu head off. The vampire stumbled, and I slipped from his grip, landing easily on my feet. The vampire turned his back to me and let out a roar so loud my ears started to ring. And I knew in that moment that Allcot had lost all sense of control. If I didn't do something, Dax was going to die. Allcot would end him and not even blink an eye.

Without hesitation, I lifted my knife and lunged forward, jamming the knife into the left side of Allcot's back.

The vampire instantly froze, and I knew I'd hit my mark. "Move one muscle, Allcot," I whispered, "and I'll end you once and for all."

Chapter Seven

"Jesus," I heard Dax say from the other side of the room.

"You're going to regret this, Kilsen," Allcot said in a voice so low and controlled I barely heard him.

"Probably," I said, forcing myself to act unconcerned. "But in the meantime, this is keeping you from doing anything stupid." *Like killing my partner.*

Allcot snarled, and even though he was holding himself perfectly still, I could almost feel his rage vibrating inside him. And the fact that the vampire had frozen in place meant the knife was perilously close to nicking his heart.

I knew the blade had come within striking distance, but I hadn't actually been aiming to kill him. Christ, the shit storm that would rain down on me if I actually killed Allcot—whether he deserved it or not—would be colossal. Still, I wouldn't hesitate to do it if he went after Dax again.

Halston had gotten to her feet, and she walked up to Allcot, her dark eyes blazing as she glared at him. She looked over his shoulder at me and nodded, her frizzy gray hair bobbing with the motion. "Good work, Kilsen."

"Thanks," I said, feeling the warmth of Link's body as he leaned against my leg, showing his support.

"Impressive really," she said to Allcot this time. "The shifter and the witch took you down with the most basic of weapons and no powers. Isn't that interesting?"

A low rumble reverberated from Allcot's chest. If the situation hadn't been so serious, if Willow hadn't still been missing, I might've laughed at the absurdity of holding Allcot's life in my hands while my boss taunted him. In no scenario had I ever imagined a scene like this. And to be honest, I really didn't want any part of it. But there was no turning back now.

"What did you really come here for, Eadric?" Halston asked, her tone curious now.

"To kill you," he spat out.

Dax's gaze met mine, and confusion rolled between us. Why would Allcot want to kill Halston?

"No, you didn't." The director walked over to the window and stared out over the Irish Channel neighborhood. "You came here for answers, didn't you?"

"Yes," he spit out. "Then I'm going to kill you."

"Going to? Now that's funny." She let out a low laugh and a chill rolled over me, settling in my bones. Allcot wasn't lying. I sensed it with everything I had. She had to know that. Which meant this cat and mouse game she was playing with him was going to end up in a bloodbath. If all five of us made it out of this room alive, it would be a goddamned miracle.

"Tell me where they are," Allcot demanded.

Halston let out an exaggerated sigh. "How many times do I have to tell you? I have no idea."

"Who are 'they?'" I asked. "Pandora and the other vampire hive?"

Halston's brow furrowed. "What hive?"

"The one that took Willow and Tal," I explained, trying to catch up. "One of them led me away from the gala. The redheaded vamp I've been tracking the past week. He's a part of the hive. I'm sure of it."

"Kilsen, stop talking now," Halston ordered.

"But——" I started, and stopped when the director's glare nearly burned a hole in my head. "What am I missing?"

"You're a fucking idiot, Kilsen," Allcot said, disgust in his tone. "A rival hive didn't take Pandora. The shifters did."

"Which shifters?" Dax asked, stepping forward, alarm claiming his handsome features.

"Like you don't know. Fucking traitor." The muscles in Allcot's back rippled with tension, and he started to move forward.

"One more step, Allcot, and I'll twist this knife so hard your heart will be in ribbons," I said, my voice as hard as steel. Link let out a growl of support, and I smiled down at him.

"He's playing you, Kilsen. Go ahead and ask your partner all about the Crimson Valley wolf pack."

"He's not playing me," I said. "I know all about——"

"Kilsen!" Halston shouted. "Do not open your mouth again. Understood?"

I did, in fact, open my mouth but promptly closed it. Dax's undercover work with the Crimson Valley pack wasn't exactly classified, as Dax made no secret of the fact that he ran with them. But talking about Void business was off-limits, especially with Allcot present.

Except Willow and Tal were still missing. I couldn't just sit back and not ask questions if Allcot had some of the missing pieces. There was no choice. I had to do what I had to do. "Why do you think the shifters took Pandora?"

Halston let out a heavy sigh but didn't chastise me further. No doubt she wanted to know the answer just as much as I did, but she wanted to be the one asking the questions.

"I fucking saw them carrying her off. Do you understand what I'm telling you? Shifters got the better of my wife. The same fucking shifters your boy toy over there has been helping for months."

Without warning, Allcot lurched forward and flew, actually flew through the office, and once again grabbed Dax by the throat. "If anything happens to her, I'll rip your limbs off one by one and just stand there while I watch you bleed out. Do you hear me?"

Dax wouldn't have been able to answer even if he tried. Allcot had cut off his ability to even breathe, much less talk. Instead, my partner kicked out, fiercely aiming for Allcot's crotch. He missed and Allcot let out a low, sinister laugh. "You can keep— Fuck!"

The vampire dropped Dax, then reached up and pulled the dart out of his neck. He glared at Halston, who was still holding the tranq gun, and then his eyes rolled into the back of his head just before he collapsed to the floor.

Dax climbed to his feet, rubbing at his neck. "You couldn't have done that a little sooner?"

"Why?" Halston asked. "Kilsen had a knife practically in his heart. I had no idea he was crazy enough to risk death just to strangle you."

I stared at Allcot's limp body and tried to process what he'd been saying. But none of it made sense. How had the shifters gotten to Pandora in the middle of all those vampires? I glanced back up at Halston. "What happened while I was out tracking that vampire?"

Her eyebrows shot up and disappeared under her frizzy gray hair. "Didn't Marrok fill you in?"

"Not really. He was engaged in his own altercation. He didn't see anything."

She cleared her throat. "Well, that is unfortunate, isn't it?"

Dax and I shared another confused glance as the director picked up the phone and ordered security to take Allcot to a holding cell.

Not five seconds later, two large security guards rushed in and dragged Allcot out.

I turned to Dax. "Do you have any idea what he was talking about? Do you think the Crimson Valley wolves have anything to do with this?"

"I don't…" He grimaced as he shook his head. "They might when it comes to Pandora. The truce between them and the Cryrique vampires is perilous at best. I'm not aware of any plan that was in the works, but if she pissed one of them off, they might've gone rogue and taken her."

They'd abducted Allcot himself only a few months ago. Not long after, Dax had negotiated a truce. The shifters would stop their attacks on the Cryrique as long as the Cryrique stayed away from their pack.

"They would have if Allcot's been experimenting again," I said.

And when I say experimenting, I mean running clinical drug tests on shifters. The Cryrique was actively developing healing drugs for all types of paranormals as well as dabbling in recreational concoctions. And while healing drugs might seem noble on the surface, their testing methods weren't one hundred percent ethical. It was always all about profits when it came to the Cryrique. It didn't matter to the pack that the shifters in question had been willing participants. In the pack's eyes, their members had been exploited.

"I haven't heard any rumors of that." Dax frowned. "In fact, I haven't heard any rumors of anything for a few weeks." He rubbed a hand over his forehead. "Fuck."

Fuck was right. There was always, *always,* something going on with the pack. If he hadn't heard anything, they'd cut him off and were intentionally keeping him in the dark. "Dax, you have to go now. Get back to the pack and find out if they know anything about Wil, Talisen, or Pandora."

"Do you need backup?" Halston asked him.

Dax shrugged. "I can probably handle it on my own, but backup is always a plus." His gaze landed on me, one eyebrow raised in question.

"I can't do it." I flopped down into one of the metal chairs the director kept around to remind us we shouldn't be sitting on the job, and Link settled at my feet. "They'll never talk if they think I'm sniffing around." I didn't have the best reputation with the rogue-shifter population. Ever since I kicked their asses and helped Allcot escape their hostage games, I'd been labeled a vamp sympathizer. The sad part of their hasty judgment was that if the situation had been reversed and the vamps had been holding a shifter hostage, I would've done the same for them. But they only saw what they wanted to see.

"She's right. I'll take Sebastian with me," Dax said.

Halston nodded and once again picked up the phone, this time to call the shifter in question.

Dax moved to stand in front of me. "Are you doing all right?"

I stood and let out a strangled laugh. "Me? What about you? Allcot did his best to choke the life out of you."

He shook his head. "No, he didn't. He just wanted to hurt me." Dax lifted his arm and nodded to his wrist. The skin was bruised purple, but judging by the fact that he was able to move it, his bones had already healed. Ultrafast healing was quite the perk of being a shifter. It also meant other supernaturals never hesitated to snap a shifter's bones. It caused the maximum amount of pain and didn't result in any permanent damage. At least not physically. "If he'd wanted me dead," Dax continued, "you'd be calling the coroner right about now. If he'd been serious, not one of us could've stopped him."

"You're right," I said, a tiny bit of tension draining from my shoulders. "I've just never seen Allcot like that before. It seemed as if he'd legitimately lost his mind. I guess I thought he wasn't thinking clearly."

"He wasn't. That's what happens to us poor bastards when our girls are in danger." He reached up and gently brushed a lock of hair out of my eyes. Then he bent down and pressed a gentle kiss on my forehead.

On the surface, the gesture was sweet, chaste even. But my body responded instantly to his touch, and I had to stop myself from swaying into him, from wrapping my arms around him and burying my face in his chest right there in front of our boss.

No, Phoebe, I chastised myself. There was a reason I'd put the brakes on the physical side of our relationship. Dax was a damned good partner, and I didn't want to ruin it with romantic entanglements. So much for that. He'd just implied

I was his girl with that last statement, and my heart had fluttered like a lovesick teenager's.

I leaned back, putting distance between us, and gave him a hint of a smile. "Try not to get your ass kicked again, okay?"

He chuckled. "I'll do my best."

Halston replaced the phone on the base, cleared her throat, and stared at us with disapproval. "Marrok, please keep it professional. Kilsen is your partner, not your girlfriend."

"Yes, ma'am," he said, his lips twitching with amusement as he kept his gaze trained on me.

Halston's tone turned clipped as she added, "Sebastian will meet you in the lobby in five minutes."

This time he glanced over at the director, giving no indication he was bothered by her chastisement. "What do you want Phoebe to do?"

"Kilsen will interview Allcot after the tranquilizer wears off."

"Sounds… frustrating," Dax said, giving me a look of sympathy. "Try not to stake his ass before he gives you something good to work with." Then he winked and walked out of the office.

"That relationship will eventually bring you both down," Halston said.

I lifted my chin in defiance. "There is no relationship."

The director snorted. "Right." When I didn't respond, she pressed her lips into a thin line and shook her head. "Don't say I didn't warn you."

Ignoring her advice, I asked, "Why did you keep ordering me to stop talking to Allcot?"

Her head snapped up and she pierced me with her dark

gaze. "All matters that pertain to the Crimson Valley wolves are classified. You know that. We don't discuss Void business with anyone, especially not Eadric Allcot."

I flinched at her sharp tone but stood my ground. "I know that. But Willow and Talisen are missing, and so is Pandora. Don't you think those two things are related?"

Halston let out a long sigh and sank into her chair, leaning back as she studied me. "Of course they are related. But do you honestly think Allcot is going to work with the Void in good faith?"

I lifted one shoulder in a half shrug. "He might. This is Pandora we're talking about."

The director's eyes narrowed, then she wrinkled her nose in distaste. "How can you be such a skilled witch and yet be so naïve?"

Anger prickled down my spine, and I clenched my fists in an effort to keep from lashing out at her. I knew better than anyone what Eadric Allcot was capable of. Willow had been tangled up in his bullshit for the past two years, and I'd been the one right there helping her through it all.

"I can see I touched a nerve," Halston said conversationally. "You think you know how to handle him, don't you?"

"I didn't say that," I said, refusing to take her bait.

"You didn't have to." She snorted a chuckle. "Just remember, there is no one more manipulative than Allcot. No one. And if you choose to trust him, sooner or later you'll get burned."

"Message received."

She stared at me for a long moment then said, "All of your other cases have been reassigned. Your sole duty now is to find Rhoswen and bring her home. Understood?"

"What resources do I have?" I asked just to judge how serious she was taking Willow's disappearance. Willow had been an agent of the Void at one time, but she wasn't any longer. Sometimes agents who left the organization were hung out to dry when shit went down.

Halston's lips formed a thin, grim line. "Whatever it takes. With her ability, it's far too dangerous for the Void if she falls into the wrong hands."

Far too dangerous for the Void. Of course that was the reason I was being given full support. It didn't matter that Willow's life was in danger. Or that she'd been a valued member of the Void. Or that she was a fae in the hands of some random vampire or shifter. No, it mattered that she had the ability to turn vampires into daywalkers, and the Void wanted to keep that little secret tightly under wraps. Typical. But all that mattered was I had the full weight of the Void behind me. "Thank you," I said and signaled for Link to follow me. "I'll be in the research center until Allcot regains consciousness."

The director nodded, and as Link and I left, I was already texting my contacts back at the Cryrique compound.

Chapter Eight

$\mathcal{D}$ax pulled his ten-year-old Trooper onto the dirt road that led to a large white plantation home. The old house was off of River Road, south of New Orleans, and surrounded by moss-draped oak trees. He eyed the dozen beat-up cars parked out front and knew something was going down.

"Looks like we're in for an interesting evening," Sebastian said, tapping his thigh in a steady beat.

The tension rolling off him had Dax itching to escape the truck. Both of them were wired, and if they kept feeding off each other's energy, neither one of them was going to be able to play it cool with the rest of the pack.

Dax blew out a breath as he pulled the Trooper to a stop and eyed the large plantation. Light glowed from all the windows, and two shifters were stationed out front.

Steeling himself, ready for anything, even the possibility that the pack had abducted the two fae, he climbed out of the

Trooper and moved with purpose up the walk, Sebastian right behind him.

"Marrok. No one said you'd be here." A shifter Dax knew only as Stone eyed him.

"I must've forgotten to RSVP," Dax said dryly, not slowing down as he climbed the front steps.

"Hold up. Who's the pretty boy?" Stone jerked his head toward Sebastian. "Your new boyfriend?"

"Sounds like you need a date, Stone." Dax said. "Want me to set you two up?"

Sebastian let out a low growl, making it clear to them both he didn't appreciate the exchange.

"Relax, pretty boy. I'm already taken," Stone said as he let out a short laugh and opened the door for them, waving them in. "Good luck in there."

Dax frowned, wondering why the hell they'd need luck but not asking. He'd find out soon enough. He walked through the entrance and was surprised to hear only a faint murmur from somewhere in the back of the house. When a dozen or so shifters were milling about at the compound, usually the decibel level was somewhere around a dull roar.

"Do you have a plan?" Sebastian asked, following Dax through the house.

"Not yet." Dax made his way to the back of the house, scanning the empty rooms as his heavy boots echoed on the old hardwood floors. Finally he came to a stop at the end of the hall and pushed the door to the left open.

Inside, Nova Bandu, the leader of the Crimson Valley wolf pack, was at the front of the room, scribbling on a blackboard. He wore his dark hair in a man-bun, and he had at least three months' worth of beard growth. His jeans were rolled up, and he was sporting suspenders over his plain white

T-shirt. The shifter was easily over sixty years old if Dax remembered correctly, but thanks to the antiaging properties of the shifter gene, he looked like every other thirtysomething hipster in New Orleans. Twenty or so Crimson Valley wolves were seated in folding chairs, most of them leaning forward and hanging on Bandu's every word.

Bandu turned around as he said something about canvassing the Bywater district. But when his gaze landed on Dax, he stopped abruptly and called, "Marrok! There you are. I was wondering where you'd gotten off to." He gestured to an open seat in the front row. "We saved a seat for you."

"You hang out back here," Dax said under his breath to Sebastian. "Don't ask them about anything, just listen and see what you can pick up."

"Got it." Sebastian took a seat in the back row next to two shifters who looked bored as hell. Good, he thought. If they weren't interested in whatever Bandu had to say, maybe they'd find something more interesting to talk about.

A scattering of murmurs traveled through the pack as everyone watched Dax move to the front of the room. Before Dax claimed his chair, he scanned the shifters and let out a small sigh of relief when he spotted Leo and Dali on the far side of the room. At least the two of them had managed to stay out of trouble.

"Where were we?" Bandu asked, staring at his blackboard.

"You wanted a group of us to canvass the Bywater," one of the shifters called out.

"Right." Bandu turned around and eyed Dax. "We heard about your friends, the fae couple. We're making a plan to search the city. If they're still here, we'll find them."

Dax's eyebrows rose. "Really? Why?"

Bandu's brow furrowed in confusion. "Why? Why not?"

"Don't get me wrong, I think it's exactly the right thing to do. But have you thought this through? Tangling with the vampires means walking headfirst into this simmering war."

"You said it yourself, Marrok. It's the right thing to do." Bandu turned back around—but not before Dax noted the irritation in the leader's expression—and continued to write down the various neighborhoods of New Orleans on the blackboard.

Dax kicked his feet out and smiled to himself. He'd wondered if Bandu was the real deal. The shifter leader had positioned himself as a man of conviction, ready to put himself on the line to do the right thing, to push boundaries to right any kind of wrong. The entire war against the vampires was based off of trying to stop the vampires from exploiting vulnerable shifters. It was good to know his convictions included helping species other than his own.

After Bandu identified the five neighborhoods where a vampire was most likely to locate a hideout, he assigned all the shifters in the room to canvassing shifts, even Sebastian, whom he welcomed without suspicion. Then he had each of them pledge to recruit a few friends to help them search for possible hideouts.

"That's it for now," Bandu said. "Those of you headed out now, don't forget to stop by the arsenal to arm yourselves."

The shifters all got to their feet and started to move out of the room. More than one placed a hand on Dax's shoulder in a gesture of support as they brushed past him. Once the pack cleared out of the room, Bandu took a seat next to Dax.

"I'm glad you made it," Bandu said.

"Why didn't anyone call me?" Dax asked.

Bandu studied him for a moment, but instead of answering, he stood. "I want to show you something."

His interest piqued, Dax stood and followed Bandu into an adjoining room.

Bandu flipped the light on and Dax sucked in a sharp breath. Three of the walls were covered with brutal images of supernatural beings, each of them mangled and soaked in blood. The fourth wall had images of young shifters, all of them with haunted expressions.

"What's this all about?" Dax asked, dread creeping into his chest cavity, unsure if he really wanted to know.

"All of these people?" Bandu nodded to the ones who'd been brutally beaten or murdered. "They were attacked by vampires. Used as food or ripped to shreds for daring to protect someone else from becoming food."

Dax's stomach rolled. "How…" He swallowed the bile rising in the back of his throat. "Where did all these pictures come from?"

"We have someone who works in forensics," Bandu said, his expression flat and void of any emotion. "I asked for a running record. He sends them over once a month." The leader walked over to a small desk and picked up a thick manila envelope. "This is last month's delivery. Want to wager how many pictures are in here?"

"There aren't that many attacks in New Orleans," Dax said. "Kilsen and I—"

"No, they aren't all in New Orleans," Bandu agreed with a nod. "They're from the entire state. Because you and Kilsen are so good at your jobs, the vampires in this town have taken to terrorizing the surrounding areas. They know you don't go out into the bayou or up to Baton Rouge. Did you really think your work had cut down the number of attacks?"

Actually, Dax had thought exactly that, but he wasn't about to admit it now. Instead, he asked, "You think the attacks are coming from the Cryrique vampire hive?"

"Maybe not the actual hive. Allcot is pretty strict about his inner circle's behavior. But Cryrique is the largest vampire employer in the area. We have reason to believe there are groups within the organization that are actively seeking unwilling feeders."

Nausea hit Dax as he took in Bandu's theory. "You're sure all these attacks are from vampires?"

Bandu walked over to the closest wall and pointed to puncture wounds on one of the victims. Then another and another. "Vampire marks on each victim."

Dax curled his hands into fists as pure rage seared through his veins. He was certain that if one of Allcot's vampires crossed his path right at that moment, he'd be compelled to rip him limb from limb.

Bandu walked over to the one wall full of people staring back at him. "And these?" He trailed his fingers over the glossy black-and-white photos. "They're all survivors. Living with the memory of an attack."

"That can't be all of them," Dax ground out. "Someone is attacked practically daily."

"You're right about that. There are far too many for this one wall. There are probably enough to plaster this entire house. But these are the worst. These are the ones I chose to remind myself what we're fighting for." Bandu's tone was full of righteous conviction as he continued, "For justice, for peace of mind, for freedom to roam the city without fear."

Dax moved to the middle of the room and took in the terror reflected back at him in the photos. He'd known vampires were a threat. Not all of them, but enough that

70

New Orleans had become a city fraught with danger. It was why he and Phoebe had jobs at the Void. They were responsible for keeping the city safe. But clearly they weren't. Not even close.

Disappointment and disgust coiled in his gut. How had he been fooling himself this entire time? He let out a curse and shook his head as if that would somehow dislodge the photos from his brain.

"It's a lot to take in all at once," Bandu said.

Dax nodded. "There's no doubt about that."

"I just wanted you to see what feeds my conviction."

"Why?" Dax asked, giving Bandu his full attention. "Why me?"

"Because I want you to be my second. I need a strong shifter who can mobilize the pack when I'm not around. Who will know how to handle delicate situations and deal with pack politics." Bandu smirked. "I figure working at the Arcane gives you special insight into dealing with that sort of thing."

"That's probably true," Dax agreed. But he sure as hell didn't know how he felt about being Bandu's beta. He'd only come into the Crimson Valley pack in order to gain information about the missing vampires. He'd gotten almost nowhere on that front, because the moment he'd joined the pack, the attacks had pretty much stopped. Dax was certain it was because he'd been outed as an Arcane agent fairly quickly, but they hadn't kicked him out. Halston had insisted he stick around and keep his ear to the ground for any new activities that might be brewing.

The only problem was, in the past few months he'd started to respect Bandu. The shifter was a man of conviction, and while his earlier attempts at vigilante justice had been misguided at best, the pack had since taken to providing free security to the city. It had turned out to drastically lower the rate of attacks, and Dax had started to think of the pack as noble in their attempts to do something positive.

On the other hand, if Bandu was hiding something or decided the pack would take it upon themselves to avenge the men and women in the photos, if Dax took the beta position, he'd be the first one to know when the shit hit the fan.

"What do you say, Marrok? Ready to join the cause?" Bandu asked.

Dax turned and stared the other man in the eye, wondering when exactly he'd started to admire the other shifter. Then he held out his hand. "I'd be honored."

Bandu's lips spread into a huge grin as he clasped Dax's hand in his. "Welcome aboard. You're not going to regret this."

Dax nodded and prayed the other shifter was right.

Chapter Nine

$\mathcal{I}$ walked down the stark white hall and craned an ear, listening for the steady sounds of activity one usually found in the Void building. But the only thing I heard was the tap, tap, tap of Link's nails on the tile floor. I glanced down at Willow's wolf. "Where do you think everyone is?"

The shih tzu put his head down and kept moving.

Some help he was. Still, I was soothed by his presence. With Willow missing, he made me feel connected to her. And I was certain that wherever she was, she was soothed by the knowledge that I'd take care of him for as long as needed. Images of Willow and Tal separated and locked in that basement once again took over my thoughts, and I scowled. Where the hell were they? The room hadn't been anything I'd recognized—certainly not any room I'd ever seen at Cryrique, and I'd seen a fair number of the hidden dungeons.

It wasn't out of the realm of possibility that someone from Cryrique had taken Tal and Willow, but after Allcot's performance that morning, I didn't really believe it. I'd already crossed Allcot off my mental suspect list. He was way too erratic and out of control to be the mastermind of whatever had gone down at the gala the night before.

But if not Cryrique, then who? And what would they do to Tal and Willow to get what they wanted? The word torture floated in my mind, and I quickly shut down that train of thought. There was no time to worry about what might be happening. My one and only job was to find them.

I quickened my pace and strode into the research center. Rows of unmanned computer stations filled the room. I stopped dead in my tracks. "What the hell? Where the fuck is everybody?"

No answer, but my phone buzzed and I quickly retrieved the message I'd been waiting for. It was Nicola, Pandora's half sister.

It's true. A small pack of shifters carried Pandora off. I saw it with my own eyes. If someone is trying to blame her disappearance on vampires, they are dead wrong.

I quickly texted back. *Anyone know anything about Willow and Talisen's whereabouts?*

There was a long pause, then she responded with one word. *No.*

Frustration clouded my brain, and it was all I could do to stop myself from chucking my phone against the wall. But I needed the damned thing. Killing it would only eat up more of my precious time. Instead, I jabbed at the letters as I typed in, *You're sure? Dax said one of the Cryrique vamps saw an unknown vampire carry them off.*

My phone started ringing almost instantly, and Nicola's face popped up on the screen. "Kilsen," I answered.

"What exactly did Dax hear about Willow and Talisen?" she demanded.

"Just what I said in the text. He told me a couple of Cryrique vamps saw them carted off by some other vamps they didn't know."

"Dammit. Rival hive?" she asked.

"I have no idea. Dax isn't even here. Do you have someone in mind who could be the culprits?"

"More than I can count." She let out an exaggerated sigh. "Listen, Allcot is off doing God knows what—"

"He's here at the Void building," I interjected. If I was going to build a rapport with them to find Willow, lying wasn't going to fly. They'd know soon enough where he'd been. "We had to um... neutralize him for a bit."

There was silence over the line. Then Nicola whispered, "Fuck me. This is a cluster of epic proportions."

"You can say that again. Listen, Nicola, the tranq dart was unavoidable. As soon as he calms down, I'm sure the director will—"

"Don't worry about it. I'm certain he's... over the edge right now. I'll keep his goons in line as long as I can. But, Phoebe?"

"Yes?"

"Make sure your director lets him out soon or else I'll come for him myself." She paused for just a moment then cleared her throat. "My sister is missing, and Eadric is our best chance of finding her."

"Understood," I said. She was right. He was the most well-connected vampire in the city. One way or another, he'd find her... but only if he wasn't locked in the basement of the Arcane building. "If you hear anything about Willow or

Talisen, anything at all, please contact me ASAP. I'll do the same if I hear anything about Pandora."

"You got it."

The line went dead and I shoved my phone back into my pocket. I glanced down at Link. "Where do you think everyone went?"

The dog took a few steps forward, glanced around, then looked back at me and tilted his head as if to say "beats me."

"Son of a biscuit." I eyed the computers that housed all the research. No doubt they were each password protected. It wasn't that I couldn't hack my way into them. I certainly could without even too much effort, but I wasn't in the habit of hacking government systems. Not if I could help it anyway. Then there was the fact that the research gurus knew where to look for stuff and had a knowledge base stored in their minds that rivaled the computers'. Because the research staff rarely got out into the field, they thrived on gossip and traded in knowledge—confidential, highly classified knowledge. And if an agent could get one of the researchers to trust her, it was like hitting pay dirt.

I had a couple of people I could count on for inside information, but since the room was deserted, I was on my own with only a shih tzu for company. I let out a sigh and sat at the nearest desk. "Time to suck it up and get to work."

Being that we were in the Void offices of the Arcane, it took me longer than usual to find a way into the system. Most computer security systems were no match for me and my witchy fingers. Unfortunately, my magical abilities had been neutralized the moment I walked through security, and I had to rely solely on my knowledge of computer systems. It was a damned good thing I'd spent a fair portion of my youth joined at the hip with my brother, the computer genius.

Seth's goofy smile flashed in my mind and that pang of sadness that always lived deep in my bones washed over me. The weight of his loss was more than I could bear, and I quickly shook my head, stuffing his memory back into the hidden chambers of my heart. Everything about his disappearance was too painful, and the best thing I could do in that moment was focus on finding Willow and Tal.

With single-minded determination, I refocused my efforts, determined to find a way into the database. My fingers ached with the effort as I continuously pounded on the keys. A thin sheen of sweat coated my forehead, and I started to wonder if the security was going to get the best of me. But just as a growl of frustration escaped my lips, the security wall vanished and the main research screen popped up on the monitor.

"Yes!" I clicked the tab that read Identity Search. Another screen came up, and I added in the meager details on the vampire we'd lost the night before. Hair color: red. Vampire age: over one hundred. He was far too strong to be a vampire of the current century. Strength: off the charts. Last known location: New Orleans. There were other input fields, but I didn't have the answers. Saying a little prayer to the gods, I hit Enter.

An hourglass cursor spun on the screen. In a matter of seconds, it disappeared and was replaced with a long list of names. Beside roughly half the names there were thumbnail pictures of the vampires. I glanced down and groaned. Forty-two pages of results. "Get comfy, Link. We're going to be here a while."

The shih tzu let out a whimper and flopped to the floor, resting his head on his paws. I knew exactly how he felt.

I'd made it through nine pages of rejects when I finally

clicked on the right record and the vampire in question stared back at me. The word CLASSIFIED was stamped across the screen, and all the information had been blurred. Only those with clearance could see the details. Luckily, the director had given me the full support of the Void on this investigation, which meant nothing was classified if I needed it. Of course, she probably expected me to go through proper channels to secure the clearance I needed, but I didn't have time for that. Better to hack my way in now and ask for forgiveness later. Especially since the entire research team seemed to be on a field trip.

Settling in, I let my fingers fly over the keys and was gratified when the classified notice vanished and the report on Carter Voelkel flashed on the screen. "I've still got it," I said to myself.

"It appears you do," a deep voice said from behind me.

Link jumped to his feet and paced behind my chair as if to guard me. In his shih tzu form, he wasn't intimidating in the least, but I appreciated the effort.

I hit the Print button then turned to give the newcomer my attention. A tall, dark-haired man dressed in a business suit was standing with his arms crossed over his chest, eyeing me with suspicion.

"Care to explain who you are and who gave you access to classified records?" he asked. A muscle in his neck pulsed, and tension practically radiated from him.

"Agent Kilsen, and I gave myself access to the records since you all seemed to be taking a siesta." I gave him a condescending smile and walked over to the copy machine to retrieve my records.

He glanced at the computer station where I'd been working. "Who gave you a clearance code?"

"The director." It was a complete lie, but I was willing to bet the director would back me up. I had a job to do, and what was a minor detail like an access code? In fact, I was willing to bet she'd be disappointed if I couldn't hack my way in. The director respected agents who could work their way through just about anything.

The man's expression hardened. "Well, Kilsen, I'm going to have to confiscate those records until I get confirmation you have the right credentials to be here."

I laughed and sat back down in front of the computer. "You can try, but I don't think you'll be successful. In any case, you can call whomever you want for confirmation. In the meantime, I'll be right here finishing my research."

He blinked. "Do you have any idea who you're speaking to?"

"Nope. And to be honest, I don't really care."

"And why is that, Kilsen?"

"Because right this minute, a vulnerable fae and her husband are missing, and if I don't find her, all hell's going to break loose in the vampire community. Now, you have two choices. You can either help me, or you can be a thorn in my side. If you choose the latter, I'll just warn you now that I fight dirty."

The man stared at me, his expression blank for a moment. Then he threw his head back and laughed.

"Laugh it up, geek boy. In the meantime, I'll be here infiltrating your files."

"I've got to give it to you. You sure are feisty." He took a seat next to me and powered the computer on. "How about we start over. I'm Razor, the research director. And normally I'd toss your ass in the cells for hacking into my system, but since it appears you're not here under nefarious motivations,

I'll just take it as a learning opportunity to tighten up the security walls."

"Whatever, man. Do what you gotta do." I gave him a cocky smile. "But I'll probably still manage to get in if I really want to."

He bowed his head. "Challenge accepted."

I shrugged, turned back to the screen, and typed in the one word that might be the key to Willow's whereabouts.

"Asier," the man said. "What do you know about that?"

"That?" I asked. "Not who?"

He shook his head. "Definitely not a who. Where did you hear that word?"

"Whoever has Willow told her they are looking forward to Asier's arrival. If Asier isn't a who, then what is it?"

"You spoke to her? How?" His eyes narrowed in suspicion and I knew I was losing him.

"Tracing spell. Now, are you going to tell me what I need to know?"

He ran a hand through his thick dark hair, taking a moment to collect himself. Then he stared me in the eye and said, "Asier is a day that comes around every four years. Paranormals who practice the old ways have a celebration and…" He grimaced and glanced away.

"Razor," I said, dread crawling up my spine. "And what?"

"Fuck." He turned and faced me. "We need to get your friend the hell out of there."

"*Friends*," I corrected, standing up, ready to fly into action. Clenching my fists, I hovered over him. "What exactly is it you're not telling me?"

"Your friends are in danger—"

"No shit, jackass. I got that part."

He pressed his lips into a thin line of impatience. "As I was trying to say, your friends are in danger of being used as an offering."

"To what? The gods?" I asked, horrified.

"Yes. Over the past couple of decades, a group of paranormals have taken to performing rituals from the ancient text. They believe that by sacrificing sacred blood to the earth they will become more powerful."

"And this happens on Asier?"

"Yes."

"What exactly qualifies as ancient blood?"

His face turned ashen white as he forced out, "Fae blood."

Chapter Ten

I stood up so quickly the force of my movement flipped the chair over. Link let out a yelp and scrambled forward. "What paranormals? Who exactly are we talking about here?"

Razor shook his head. "It's unclear."

"What the hell does that mean?" I paced up and down one of the aisles. "Don't you understand? My best friend is being held by whoever these sick bastards are, and if I don't find her, that could be her fate."

"I do understand," he said, his expression full of a strange mix of sympathy and anger. "All too well."

I paused and stared at him. His jaw was lifted, shoulders tense, and one fist was clutching a pen. But his dark eyes, they were haunted. Whatever this Asier business was, he'd seen it before. "Tell me everything you know."

Instead of answering, he spun his chair around and his fingers flew over the keyboard. Within moments, a file flashed on the screen. The name at the top read Amber Frost. He froze for a moment as he stared at the picture of the beautiful young woman associated with the report. She had long blond hair, piercing gray eyes, full red lips, and that same ethereal quality that both Willow and Tal possessed.

"She's a fae," I said. It wasn't a question.

"Was a fae." He swallowed. "She went missing just over four years ago."

"You knew her." Again, it wasn't a question. The anguish in his tone and body language said it all. Whoever this woman was to him, she'd been important and he still hadn't recovered from her disappearance.

He tore his gaze from the computer screen and turned cold, hate-filled eyes on me. "She was their last sacrifice."

His words weren't a surprise to me. Why else would he be showing me her file? "Who are they, Razor?"

"I don't fucking know." He jabbed his finger on the mouse. The printer roared to life, spitting out the record he'd pulled up for me.

"Vampires? Shifters? Witches?" I asked.

He shook his head. "Probably not witches. As far as vampires or shifters go, look for yourself. The report is right there."

I moved back to the printer, wondering why he didn't just tell me what he knew. But the minute I laid eyes on the paper, I understood. He didn't have the answer. Not a definitive one. No one did. The report indicated Amber had been drained of her blood. That was a clear indication vampires had been involved. But she'd also been ripped to shreds as if she'd been offered to a feral pack of wolves. My stomach turned, and I shook my head, forcing the image of Willow suffering the same fate from my mind.

In all my years as a vampire hunter, I'd never known one

vamp that was the slightest bit interested in carnage. They were singularly focused on blood. It was their food, their life force, and also part of their sexual gratification. It was also their preferred way to harm someone. The only exception was when a vampire went up against a fae who regularly drank liquid sunshine, a drug that made their blood taste bad to vampires. The vamps wouldn't drink from them. They were far more likely to break the fae's neck, ending the altercation quickly. Shifters were the ones known for bodily destruction when engaging in a death match.

Unless destroying a fae was part of the ritual, I didn't see vampires having any part of it. I looked up from the sheet, rage coiling in my gut. "There were never any leads?"

"Just one. A lone shifter by the name of Ezan."

I raised my eyebrows. "No pack?"

"Nope. He was ostracized by the Blue Bayou pack. In fact, they helped me hunt him down." Razor's entire body stiffened with the memory, and I had the impression I was watching a man who was right back in that moment, ready to strike. The glazed look in his eyes was a dead giveaway. Then his body started to vibrate, and he let out a piercing howl.

I wasn't afraid of him, but I took a step back, putting a bit more distance between us. I hadn't been sure if he was a witch or shifter; there was no way to tell inside the Void building. The howl set the record straight. He was a definitely a shifter and would have better than average combat skills. I was confident in my own abilities, but if he snapped out of reality, I didn't want to have to test them out on a man who should be an ally. Wanting to keep him talking, I lowered my voice and in a steady tone asked, "Did you get anything out of him? Any known associates?"

His dark eyes pierced me as his muscles flexed.

"Keep it together Razor. I'm not your enemy."

His lips curled into a snarl, but then he seemed to come back to himself because he uncurled his fists and his expression turned blank. "We never identified his associates. I was under the impression they all perished in a warehouse fire. Their remains were unidentifiable."

"Good goddess," I whispered. "Brutal."

"Not brutal enough," he said as pain flashed over his features again. "After what they did to Amber, they deserved to burn."

"And what happened to Ezan?"

"I ended him." Razor turned back to his computer and shut it down. "Made him suffer just like Amber."

In other words, he'd torn him apart and left him in pieces. "Any intel?"

The shifter shook his head slowly. "Amber was already dead, and I was too far gone to care in that moment." His haunted eyes met mine. "After learning about Willow Rhoswen's abduction, it's my only regret."

I sucked in a deep breath and slowly let it out. My only lead on Asier was one dead shifter. But he did have ties to the Blue Bayou pack. They might know something about their former member and his associates. It was only a tiny thread, but at least it was something.

"One last question," I said.

He nodded, his shoulders hunched and his face haggard as if exhaustion had set in.

"Ezan was a shifter, but you said you didn't know if the ones involved in Asier were shifters or vampires. Is there a reason to believe vampires could be involved?"

"Yes. The offering on Asier is supposed to purge and save paranormals souls. Plenty of vampires have expressed interest in the practice over the years. All desperate paranormals have. The one thing I did learn from Ezan is that his group did not discriminate. Anyone who wanted to be saved could join the cult. I've interviewed a half dozen shifters he tried to recruit and about the same number of vampires. You'll see it in the report."

I flipped through the papers in my hands and scanned the summary. Sure enough, there were about a dozen statements from various paranormals indicating Ezan had tried to recruit them to participate in some cleansing ritual. I was about to stuff the papers into a folder when one name caught my attention—Nova Bandu, the leader of the Crimson Valley wolf pack.

"I'll be damned," I whispered, my eyes widening as I read his statement. When I was done, I grinned at Razor. "You've been more help that I could've hoped for. Thank you."

"I don't know that I gave you anything useful. Four years ago, we ran into a dead end. I'm not sure anything's going to change that now."

"You'd be surprised how things start to shake out when someone's life is on the line." I shoved the paperwork into a file and snapped my fingers. "Ready, Link?"

The shih tzu hurried to my side and the pair of us strode for the door. Just before I disappeared out into the hallway, I turned back. "By the way, where was everyone today?"

"We sent them home when we learned Allcot penetrated the building."

"But you stayed?"

He shrugged. "I'm the boss."

I sent him a warm smile. "You know, Razor, I think I like you. If you ever need anything, don't hesitate to get in touch."

"Same, Kilsen. It was interesting meeting you."

After one last nod, I jerked my head and Link followed me out into the stark hallway.

MY BOOTS ECHOED on the wooden staircase as I descended into the basement of the Void building. Link followed, but when I reached the dirt floor, he stayed on the last step, unwilling to go farther into the cold, dark room. I couldn't say I blamed him. The last time he'd been down here, he'd been locked in a cage waiting for death.

"It's okay, dude. No one's going to lock you up this time," I said. "They'll have to go through me first." Because if there was one thing I knew, it was that I wouldn't let anything happen to Willow's dog. He'd be right there by my side when I finally found her.

His amber eyes flashed in the shadows as he took the final step onto the cold floor.

"Kilsen, how nice of you and the wolf to visit me," a familiar voice drawled.

I squinted in the darkness, barely making out the cell in the corner. Allcot's pale features made it easier to spot him though, and I moved forward. "You're awake."

"Have been for a while. I'm surprised no one told you that."

"They were probably letting you cool off a bit," I said, sitting on a stool against the far wall. Allcot was in the magically enhanced cell, but he was an old, powerful vampire. There was no telling what tricks he could pull. I didn't want to be too close, just in case he managed to break free. Link seemed to share my thoughts and trotted over to me, sitting at my feet.

"I'm only going to say this once," he said, the stone-cold viciousness in his voice chilling me to the bone. "Let. Me Out."

"I will," I said easily, pretending his demeanor didn't bother me at all. The fact was I fully expected that if we detained him for too long, he'd likely destroy everything and everyone in his way as he bulldozed his way out of here. "We just need to have a chat first."

His nostrils flared. "Unless you have information on Pandora, I'm not interested."

"Then it's unfortunate that I don't. But I am in charge of the investigation to find Willow and Talisen. And since the three of them went missing at the same time, it's likely the abductions are related don'tcha think?"

A tiny flash of interest lit his eyes, but he blinked and it was gone. "Open the cell, Kilsen, or I'll—"

"Tear the place down. I got it." I waved an impatient hand. "Forget it. Not until we have an understanding. The way I see it, we each have a vested interest in what happened to Pandora and Willow and Talisen. If we work together, I think we can find them faster, don't you?"

His green eyes narrowed. "Your director put me in prison and you almost killed me. Why would I work with you or the Void?"

"Because the only reason we did either of those things was because you tried to kill Marrok, and you know it."

The vampire wrapped his hands around the bars of the cells and squeezed. The iron made a high-pitched noise of distress but stayed in place. "The shifters took Pandora," he said as if that explained his actions.

"We don't know that."

"I *saw* them," he snarled.

"But what pack are they from? Marrok says it's not the Crimson Valley pack. He also says some of your vampires saw Willow and Talisen hauled off by some other vampire hive."

"Taken by two different groups. Disappearances are unrelated. Now let me out. We'll discuss restitution for my unlawful incarceration later."

I snorted out a choked laugh. "Restitution? You really are an arrogant bastard, aren't you?"

He gave me an indignant glare and opened his mouth, but I held up a hand, stopping him.

"Do you know anything about Asier?" I asked, eyeing him closely to monitor his reaction.

Allcot's normally cool expression instantly shifted into one of disgust. "That is an ancient ritual that is not tolerated here in New Orleans. No self-respecting vampire would ever engage in anything so sacrilegious."

"Why? Because the blood is offered up to the earth?"

"Do not insult me, Kilsen. Contrary to some of the unsavory opinions out there about me and my company, we actually value the sanctity of life. It's why the majority of our resources at Cryrique go to pharmaceutical research. We are dedicated to helping the paranormal community, not eradicating it of our members."

Dedicated to the bottom line was more like it. This time I held back my snort. Antagonizing him wasn't going to get me anywhere. Besides, for all of Allcot's faults, the idea that he was involved in some sort of ritual cult killing was laughable. He was right when he said the majority of the company's resources went to research. Everything he did revolved around science and profits. Reducing his customer base with ritual killings would do nothing to fatten his bank account.

"All right. You might have a point. But the fact is we're fairly certain we know that whoever has Willow and Talisen is planning on conducting a ritual on the next Asier. I don't know if Pandora is with them or not, but I'm asking that when I let you out of here that you'll cooperate with me on finding all three of them."

Allcot straightened, and although I wouldn't have thought it possible, his features turned a paler shade of white. "Asier? Are you positive?"

"I traced Willow. She said she overheard them say they couldn't wait for Asier."

"Fuck!" His hands tightened on the bars again and he yanked, causing the entire structure to bend.

My eyes widened at his impressive force. We'd locked up any number of vamps over the years, but never had we had one with that much strength.

"Get me the fuck out of here." His green eyes were unfocused, almost wild as his voice rasped with anger. "No one is going to spill Rhoswen's blood. No one."

"Do we have a deal then?" I asked, needing to know before I released him where we stood.

"Rhoswen is under my protection. You know that Kilsen." He blinked and his stone-cold businessman persona returned. "You'll work for me while we track her down."

I was afraid of that. Allcot didn't answer to anyone. "You know I work for the Void."

"And now you'll work for me. Or you will if you want your friend home safe."

Okay, that pissed me off. "You don't need to insult my abilities, Allcot. I am an experienced tracker."

"But I have the connections, and you obviously need my help or you wouldn't be negotiating with me." He took a step back from the bars and crossed his arms over his chest. His arrogance was suffocating and only got worse when he added, "You'll work for me, take it or leave it."

"One more question first," I said.

He just stared at me, waiting.

"Besides being out of your mind looking for Pandora, why did you want to kill Halston?"

His chilly facade disappeared and raw hatred laced his voice when he said, "Because that power-hungry bitch doesn't care about anything or anyone other than herself."

"I'm not sure that's true," I hedged. "She told me I had use of all the Void's resources to find Willow."

A hollow laugh escaped his lips. "Only because she's of value to the Void. If you really want to know why I threatened her, ask her sometime. Now let me out of here so we can get to work."

"On two conditions," I said. "One, don't ever touch Dax again."

Allcot's lips curved into a knowing smile. "You've got it bad for that one, don't you?"

I ignored his observation, even though it was true, and added, "You can't bail if we find Pandora first."

"I won't stop until we find the fae. You have my word on that."

"And Dax?"

That sordid smile was back, making me want to smack it off his youthful face. God, he was such a creeper. "Sure, Kilsen. Your shifter is safe from the big bad wolf."

I rolled my eyes, but I reached for the key tucked in my front pocket. Halston was going to blow a gasket when she learned about our deal. But I'd known I was going to work with Allcot before I'd ever stepped into the room. I was already convinced he had nothing to do with Willow and Tal's abduction. And Allcot had resources no other organization had. Plus roughly a half dozen of his vampires were loyal to Willow thanks to her ability to turn them into daywalkers.

The cell door swung open and Allcot strode out. Without saying a word, he flew up the stairs, leaving Link and me in the dust. I glanced down at the shih tzu. "This should be interesting."

Link let out a sharp bark and took off after the vampire, his short legs working overtime to get him up the stairs. I ran after them, relieved to finally start the hunt.

Chapter Eleven

---

*T*he moment I stepped outside the Void building, my phone buzzed and Link bounded up to me still in his shih tzu form. The text was from Dax. *Where are you?*

I typed back, *Just leaving the Void building. You?*

On my way back into the city. I should be there in twenty minutes. Meet me at the safe house? We need to talk.

That didn't sound good. *Any news on Willow?*

Not yet. This is about the pack.

I sighed, disappointed, but knew whatever it was, it'd be important. Dax was all business when he was on a case. Besides, I needed to fill him in on my new arrangement with Allcot as well. I glanced up, finding the vampire leaning against his black BMW. He had dark sunglasses hiding his eyes, but I could still see his right eyebrow arch in question. "I need to meet with Marrok before we take off."

"Do what you have to do, Kilsen. I'm headed out to find Pandora." He opened his car door and started to slide in.

"Wait!" I ran around to the driver's side and grabbed the

door handle, stopping him from pulling it shut. "Where are you going? I'll meet you there in forty-five minutes."

He pulled his glasses off, staring up at me, his eyes cold and emotionless. For a moment, I was certain he was going to call the arrangement off, but then he gave me a short nod. "Meet me at my compound. But if you're not there in one hour, I'm leaving without you."

"Okay. I'll—"

His hand shot out, knocking me back. The car door slammed shut, and Allcot took off, the wheels squealing in his haste.

"Rude ass," I mumbled as Link trotted over to me, nudging me with his nose. "I'm okay, buddy."

Another text had come in while I'd been negotiating with Allcot. This one was from the director. Four words. *What have you done?*

I ignored Halston's message and sent a reply back to Dax. *I'm on my way.*

THE ONLY SAFE house of mine that Dax Marrok knew about was just a couple of blocks from the Void building. It was in the heart of the Irish Channel, a neighborhood that at one time had been a little on the rough side and home to far too many criminal syndicates. As a result, when I'd purchased the safe house, it had been just another decaying property among many others on the street and a perfect hideout from anyone looking for me.

But these days the neighborhood was revitalizing and the house that appeared to be falling down was becoming more of a liability than an asset. And that was the only reason I'd shared the location with Marrok. Inside, it was equipped with state-of-the-art security, high-tech computers, an office, and a comfortable bed to sleep in if I felt for some reason I couldn't go home.

Today I was grateful for the office space as I studied the research files Razor had helped me find while I waited for Dax to arrive. Link was snoozing in the corner while I hunched over my desk, staring at the information collected about Asier. The highly secretive group that worshipped the event remained completely underground. They only surfaced every four years in early spring as they prepared for their ritual, which was to be held during the full moon of the fourth month. I glanced at the calendar and noted the full moon was only two days away.

Two days.

My heart sped up as a rush of adrenaline shot through my veins. The urge to arm myself with every spell and weapon I possessed and then charge out of the house on a rampage overwhelmed me. The last thing I wanted to be doing was sitting in a house, combing through research, but I sucked in a breath and forced myself to calm down. Aimlessly searching the city wasn't going to help anyone. I needed some idea of where Allcot and I should be looking.

I turned the sheet over and scanned a short paragraph indicating a tracker had infiltrated their ranks eight years ago on April twenty-fifth, but there wasn't any word on if he'd successfully thwarted their ritual plans. My eyes widened in shock when I recognized the code name.

BL4Z3R

"Blazer?" I said aloud, my voice cracking. The code name was the one my brother Seth had used for years during our hacker days and had insisted upon using for all his sensitive cases while working for the Void. There was no question that the report was referring to him. I was absolutely sure of it. I quickly read through the rest of the document, looking for any further references to BL4Z3R.

Nothing.

"Dammit." With my heart racing, I rummaged through my desk drawer and pulled out the old journal I'd tucked away long ago. It was leather bound and had a single flame carved on the cover. I ran my fingers over the flame, letting myself remember his laughing eyes and goofy smile for just a moment. Then I flipped the notebook open and turned to the month of April in the old calendar tucked inside.

The date of April twenty-first was circled, indicating it was the last day anyone had heard from my brother, a full seven days before the full moon eight years ago.

Anger and outrage seized me. How could I have not known Seth was working on a case involving a cult that practiced sacrificial rituals? I'd been told he'd messed up a routine tracking case and had just disappeared after a prominent New Orleans official was killed by a notorious vampire. There was even paperwork about the incident in his official file along with a letter condemning Seth's actions. If he hadn't disappeared, he'd have been disciplined, possibly even forced to leave the Void. He'd essentially been labeled a fuckup.

I flipped the pages in my notebook until I got to the folded piece of paper I'd received as official correspondence from the Void. Seth Kilsen had last been heard from on April twenty-first. Not the twenty-fifth, the day indicated on the Asier research.

They'd lied.

The fucking bastards had lied. What else had they

misrepresented? Had he been at fault for the death of the New Orleans official, or was that a lie too? I stood and started to pace. And the worst part was I couldn't even blame Halston. She hadn't been the director then. The revelation that my employer had been less than truthful shouldn't have been a surprise. I was under no illusions when it came to what the Void was capable of doing. The higher-ups could be just as shady as Allcot and his Cryrique minions.

But to *lie* and disparage Seth's reputation while keeping such vital information from me, their number one tracker, it was unforgiveable. Of course, I hadn't actually been a tracker then. Seth's disappearance had been the main catalyst for me even joining the Void. I'd wanted to clear the Kilsen name. Prove we were decent witches.

Still, someone in that building knew there was more than what they'd told me, and no one had bothered to fill me in. Something had happened to Seth when he infiltrated the group eight years ago. If the reports were true and the group only popped up every four years, then had I known about the sacrificial rituals four years ago, I'd have stopped at nothing to find the secret society, spare the fae sacrifices, and discover exactly what happened to my brother. With any luck, I'd have taken the society down in the process. Willow and Talisen would've never been targeted, never been abducted, and no one would be in danger of being ripped to shreds by some crazy cult of paranormals looking to have their souls saved.

Darkness filled me as anger took over, creeping into all the empty places of my heart, pushing out the sadness and the small thread of hope that I might still find Seth someday despite the years since his disappearance.

"Phoebe?" Dax's deep voice filled the small office. I

jerked my head up, startled to find my partner and Link in wolf form standing next to him. When had Link shifted?

"Where'd you come from?" I snapped and then grimaced when I heard my sharp tone. "Sorry, you just surprised me. I didn't hear you or the alarm indicators."

The safe house was a fortress, outfitted with cameras, audio, security alarms. There was even a small warning bell that was supposed to go off anytime someone made their way up the walk.

"They went off. I'm surprised you didn't hear them," Dax said, his eyebrows pinched together as he studied me. "What's got you so wound up?"

I opened my mouth to explain, then closed it and shook my head. I wasn't even sure where to start. Link moved across the room and nudged my leg, letting me know he was there if I needed him. How many times had I seen him do that with Willow? More than I could count.

Dax stood in the doorway of my office, so strong and solid and real. Something inside me broke, letting loose long-buried pain and fear. After the stress of the past twenty-four hours, I could no longer control my emotions. Shaking, I stood and walked over to him, placing my hands on his broad chest. "You have no idea how glad I am to see you right now."

Without hesitation, he wrapped his arms around me and pulled me in close. "What happened?"

I let out a choked laugh. "My best friend been kidnapped. What else is there to say?" My words were a cop-out, but I didn't know how to talk about Seth. Not yet. Not until I knew more.

He tightened his hold on me and pressed a soft kiss to the

top of my head. "Why do I have the feeling there's something more going on?"

Dax knew me far too well. Certainly the disappearance of a best friend was enough to rattle anyone. But I was a tracker, an agent of the Void. I didn't rattle easily. "There is, but I…" I didn't know what else to say.

"I'm here," he said, tightening his hold on me. "Whatever it is, we'll handle it. Just like we're going to find Willow and Talisen. One way or another, we're going to find them."

I pressed my face into his chest and prayed he was right. "Dax," I said, pulling back to look him in the eye, determined to try to explain myself. But the tenderness I saw there took my breath away, and my words got clogged in my throat.

"What is it?" He brushed a lock of my dark hair out of my eyes and tucked it behind my ear. The gesture was so simple, so sweet, and so fucking normal it almost brought me to my knees.

"I… Shit." All reason fled. I reached up, buried my hand in his thick dark hair, and pulled him down as I pressed up on my toes. Our lips met, and all the stress, worry, and fear swirling inside me numbed. All I knew was Dax and his hot lips on my mine, giving me this one moment of reprieve, a place to lose myself among the chaos.

"Jesus, Phoebe," Dax said with a growl as he backed me up against the wall. "You taste so dammed good."

I hooked one leg around his hips and ground into him, craving every inch of his long lean body. I'd been starving for him over the past two months and I hadn't even known it.

He responded by slipping his hand down to my hip, then my thigh, before moving it up to cup my ass. I let out a soft sigh of pleasure and deepened the kiss, completely lost in his woodsy scent. He smelled faintly of cypress and earth and what could only be described as sunshine. Intoxicating.

Dax tore his mouth away from mine and moved his lips to my neck, nipping and scraping his teeth over my skin while his thumb teased one of my nipples though my thin T-shirt. "Christ, I want you so bad right now."

I let my head fall to the side, giving him easier access to my neck and said, "Yes, now."

Without hesitation, he picked me up, and I wrapped my legs around his waist as he started to head toward the bedroom in the back. He'd just kicked open the bedroom door when I finally heard the low buzz of the security alert followed by the crash of the front door as it flew open and banged into the hallway wall. Link's sharp bark filled the tiny house, adding to the chaos.

Before I could even untangle myself from Dax, Allcot was there right behind Dax, Link standing calmly beside him as if Allcot were some sort of wolf whisperer.

Traitor, I thought.

Allcot's deep green eyes glinted at me. "Interesting. I guess this is what you meant when you said you needed to 'talk to Marrok.'"

Dax and I sprang apart. He stepped in front of me, shielding me from the vampire as if he'd already torn my clothes off. "How the fuck did you find this place?"

Allcot gave Dax an impatient smile. "I know everything that goes on in this town. Did you two really think I didn't know where your hideouts are? Or how to penetrate them?"

"Dammit, Allcot!" I straightened my T-shirt and stepped out from behind Dax, my body suddenly cold from the loss of his heat. "What the hell do you think you're doing just barging in here? I said I'd meet you back at your mansion."

"Meet him?" Dax asked, his eyebrows pinched in confusion. "I thought he was locked up at the Void."

"I let him out," I said, pressing two fingers to my temple. "We're combining forces to find Willow, Tal, and Pandora."

"What?" Dax said, his voice almost a growl. "Did you forget the part about vampires abducting your best friend?"

Allcot took a step forward and bared his fangs at my partner. "Are you saying my people took the fae couple?"

"Didn't they?" Dax shot back, his muscles bulging as if he was on the verge of turning into a wolf. "It's the perfect crime. Stage a fake abduction of your consort, take the fae, and pretend you know nothing about it. Then you have the fairy under your thumb and you can run tests on her, turn all your crew into daywalkers, and never have to worry about a rival getting ahold of her."

"Nice story, wolf. But if I wanted Rhoswen under my thumb, it would've happened a long time ago. You should try looking a little closer to home for answers."

"What the fuck are you talking about?" Dax demanded.

"Ask Nova Bandu," Allcot said, a chill in his tone.

"You're full of shit." Dax took another step forward, but I put my hand out, pressing my palm to his chest.

"No, Dax. We don't have time for this."

His dark eyes blazed with fury as he stared down at me. "We had all the time in the world five minutes ago before your favorite vampire walked in, didn't we, Kilsen?"

"Favorite vampire…?" Using all the pent-up frustration still strumming through me, I shoved him, sending him stumbling through the threshold of the bedroom door. "What the fuck, Marrok? Jesus. That was uncalled for."

"So was releasing the vampire who tried to kill me."

I closed my eyes and shook my head. "Please don't do this now, Dax. We have work to do."

"Not with Allcot," he said through clenched teeth.

"I don't have time for this bullshit." Allcot turned on his heel and headed back toward the front door.

"Wait!" I called and ran after him. "Why did you come here? I thought we were meeting at your mansion."

He stepped through the front door but paused and glanced back at me. "I have a lead that can't wait." Allcot stared over my shoulder, his eyes narrowed in a glare, and I knew that Dax had followed me. "You're either with me or you're with him."

"Give me just a few minutes. I need to grab my weapons." There'd been no thought process, no weighing the risks, no second-guessing. Wherever Allcot was headed, I was going with him.

"Two minutes," Allcot said. "I'll be in the car."

"Phoebe, no," Dax said from behind me. "Don't do this. The Crimson Valley pack is out in full force looking for Willow and Tal. We don't need Eadric Allcot and whatever strings come with his help."

"Link, wait here," I ordered, and the wolf obediently sat next to the open front door. "Good boy," I said as I turned and ran back to my desk. "Do they know anything about the redheaded vampire?"

"No."

"Or the shifters that took Pandora?"

"They don't think shifters took her," he said. "They think it's a rival hive."

I scoffed. "Right. Because some other group of vampires would actually be crazy enough to take Allcot's lover? He'd annihilate them and the entire vampire community would back him up."

"We're talking about monsters who kill people for their blood, Phoebe. They don't have a conscience."

I shoved the files I'd been researching into a messenger bag and reached into the desk for yet another spelled dagger. "You don't really believe that, do you? That all vampires are monsters?"

He shrugged. "Maybe."

I shook my head. "You know that's what a lot of people think about shifters, right?"

"I know what they think. But I also know that shifters are loyal to humans. Do you have any idea what Bandu's entire mission is here in New Orleans?" He didn't give me a chance to reply before he continued. "Bandu has turned the pack into keepers of the city."

"What does that mean, 'keepers of the city'?" I asked, frowning at him.

"Protectors, Phoebe. They're out there right now combing the city for Willow and Talisen, and they won't hesitate to interfere if a vampire steps out of line. People might think we're monsters, but soon they'll realize we're the only thing standing between them and a lifetime of being persecuted by vampires."

I gaped at him. "Dax, don't you realize that's what the Arcane is for, the reason we work for the Void?"

"And don't you see it's not working?" he shot back, pulling his phone out of his pocket. After tapping the screen a few times, he shoved the device at me. "See all these photos? They're of vampire victims. The ones we couldn't save."

I took a step back, eyeing him wearily. "Dax, I know there's a vampire problem. There's a shifter problem too. But taking sides right now isn't going to help us get Willow back. I need to go. Allcot—"

"No! You can't go with him. Can't you see it's all a setup? Didn't you hear what I said to him?"

I'd heard. The problem was I didn't believe it. Allcot wasn't pretending to be crazed about Pandora's disappearance. That fear in his eyes, it had been real. The reason I knew that was because Allcot was a cocky bastard, and in all the years I'd known him, I'd never seen him look desperate. And that's what I'd witnessed this morning. "I'm going, Dax. I have to."

"Phoe—"

"No! Listen, there's a sacrificial ritual that is happening in two days and involves the draining of fae blood. It's carried out during an event called Asier and is supposed to save supernatural souls, vampires and shifters alike. Or at least that's what they seem to think. That's what Willow overheard."

Confusion flashed in his dark eyes. "Draining of fae blood?"

"That's right. That's why they have Willow. So when I say I don't have time for this, I mean it. I'm going with Allcot. I'll be in touch."

Dax was far from convinced, and he shook his head, anger rolling off him in waves. "This is a mistake, Phoebe. He's dangerous. If you walk out that door, I can't be your backup on this. I can't protect you."

Frustration coiled tightly in my gut. "I don't have a choice."

"Yes, you do." He strode over to me and placed his hands on my cheeks, his determined expression staring down at me.

"Choose, Phoebe. You're either with Allcot on this or you're with me. It can't be both."

I blinked up at him. "Are you being serious right now? You want me to choose between working with you or Allcot?"

"That's what I'm saying," he said, softening his tone as his eyes pleaded with me to see reason. "He can't be trusted. You must see that. Choose, Phoebe. Say you'll stay with me. We'll find Willow together. With the help of the Crimson Valley pack, I know—"

"I'm sorry, Dax," I said, words thick with regret. "I choose Allcot."

Chapter Twelve

ax stared at the door, unable to process what had just happened. Had he really demanded Phoebe choose between him and Allcot? Jesus, what a fucking idiot he was. Of course she'd chosen the vampire. He was powerful with plenty of connections and Dax had just behaved like a controlling ass, not the type of person Phoebe Kilsen was willing to suffer.

The shifter stormed back to the desk where his partner had been working when he'd arrived. He glanced around, searching for any clues, anything that would give him more insight into what she'd learned at the Void. All he found was a leather-bound book that appeared to be filled with handwritten notes about an old case and a single piece of paper that had fallen to the floor. He picked it up, noting the name at the top—Carter Voelkel. After a quick scan, he realized it was a dossier on the redheaded vampire Phoebe had tangled with the night before.

He wasn't sure how the old case fit into the current one,

but he did know that whatever Phoebe had been working on when he'd arrived had haunted her. He wasn't so arrogant as to think that she'd suddenly decided today was the day she wanted to climb back into bed with him. Something had spooked her, and she'd dealt with it by trying to lose herself in a fleeting moment of passion.

After tucking the dossier and the notebook into his pocket, he texted Phoebe a short apology, then went to fix the damaged front door, cursing the vampire the entire time. An hour later, he locked up and checked his phone. No response from Phoebe.

"Fuck." He ground his teeth together and sent Bandu a message. He needed to know if the shifter leader knew anything about Asier.

"WHAT'S THE LEAD? Where are we headed?" I asked Allcot. We were in his car, Link in the back seat as we headed south out of town.

Allcot's cool demeanor was a sharp contrast to my shaky limbs. I was still upset from my altercation with Dax. How had we gone from almost tearing each other's clothes off to my walking out on him? It was inconceivable that he'd forced me to make a choice. He worked with a shifter pack I didn't fully trust, and yet I'd never laid a guilt trip on him for his association. Willow was far too important to put personal feelings on the line. I'd work with the devil himself if it meant finding Willow before anyone harmed her.

"River Road. Nicola did her own tracing spell on Pandora," he said.

"And it worked?" I asked, turning to give him my full

attention. Tracing spells were rarely successful when they involved vampires. Witches had a hard time connecting with their distinct energy. However, Nicola and Pandora were half sisters, so that would give Nicola an edge while working the spell.

"Yes and no." He sped up, his impatience obvious in his jerky movements. "Nicola couldn't connect with her mentally, but she did see an image of her in a house—a house I recognized."

"That's… fortuitous," I said.

His lips curved into a ghost of a smile that didn't reach his eyes. "Sometimes being a century old pays off in ways one wouldn't expect."

It was strange to hear him refer to himself as being a hundred years old. My research had told me he'd been turned when he was only twenty-two. Only, the vampire didn't look a day over seventeen. If it hadn't been for his enormous ego and commanding presence, he could've ended up one of those vampires doomed to repeat high school for eternity. Instead, he was the head of the most powerful vampire organization in the country, perhaps the world.

"River Road, huh? I assume that means one of the old plantations then?"

He nodded.

"That doesn't seem a little careless to you?" I asked, trying to figure out why anyone would hide a notorious vampire in a house on a road that was heavily traveled by tourists. River Road was home to a dozen plantations that were open to the public for tours. "I assume this one is a private residence?"

"It was. It's been empty for the past forty years. Or it was empty." That chilling expression was back on his face, and I had no doubt he was imagining the slow death of whoever had abducted Pandora.

"Did Nicola see anyone else with her?" I asked. "Willow or Talisen?"

"No."

My heart sank a little, but I wasn't surprised. Willow hadn't seen Pandora either.

Allcot yanked the wheel, and we turned onto River Road. He sped up, taking the curves as if we were flying around a speedway.

I tightened my grip on the door handle and secretly wished he'd go even faster. The vampire's reflexes were legendary. If anyone could maintain control of a car, especially one as nice as his BMW, it was him.

Suddenly Allcot took a left turn down a tree-lined gravel road. The vegetation was overgrown, and when the house came into view, it was no surprise to find the paint was peeling, the porch was sagging, and most of the windows were broken. The grand old dame's glory days were definitely behind her.

Allcot slammed on the brakes, causing the car to skid to a stop. A second later, he was out of the BMW, moving so fast toward the house he was little more than a blur. I let Link out of the back seat. He immediately ran off to inspect the grounds while I took my time, glancing around at the surroundings. There were partial tire tracks in the mud at the edge of the gravel drive. Someone had left an empty forty-ounce bottle of Bayou Reserve, the malt liquor heavily favored by the New Orleans shifter population, on the porch, and there was a pile of cigarette butts in a bucket in the neglected raised flowerbed. The place might appear to be deserted, but shifters had definitely been here in the recent past. The cigarettes and the beer bottle said it all. Vampires didn't smoke, and if they drank they indulged in red wine and fine spirits.

I paused on the porch, my skin prickling. Something wasn't right. But I couldn't put my finger on what it might be. An eerie feeling washed over me, and I scanned the area one more time.

Nothing. No shifters. No vamps. No witches.

Still, the feeling only intensified. I reached for my dagger, which was tucked into my waistband, with one hand and grabbed my sun agate with the other. If a shifter, vampire, or fellow witch came after me, I was prepared.

"Link," I called.

The wolf appeared from behind the house and jumped up onto the porch.

"Keep guard on the house. If you see anyone, warn us."

The wolf started to pace the porch, and I took that as a sign he'd understood my instructions.

I strode into the house, the spongy wood floors creaking under my weight. It was easy to see the place had been beautiful in its day, with the delicate floral wallpaper and sweeping grand staircase. Only now the discolored wallpaper had turned yellow and the moth-eaten pink velvet couch had more holes than a honeycomb. Trash was scattered in one corner, and there was so much water damage mold was growing around the windowsills.

Careful not to touch anything, I quickly made my way from room to room. When it was clear the bottom floor was empty, I climbed the creaky stairs. The second floor was just as empty as the first. I eyed the second set of rotting stairs that led to the third floor and prayed they wouldn't collapse under my weight.

It didn't take long to find Eadric. He was standing in the doorway of one of the bedrooms, his head bowed. I made my way to him and pressed my hand to his back, knowing he would have heard me long before he felt me.

"What did you find?" I asked.

"She was here. Now she's not. They knew, Kilsen. They fucking knew Nicola cast the tracing spell."

Fear seized my heart as I thought of Willow. "They knew? How?"

"Fuck if I know. But look." He dropped his arm, giving me access to the room.

I stepped around him and let out a gasp as I read the words on the far wall.

Welcome to your living hell, Allcot. Pinned below the spray-painted words was the see-through lacy black bustier and skirt Pandora had been wearing the night before at the gala. I'd recognize the outfit anywhere. That slit was so high it was indecent. Only a vampire would have enough gall to try to pull it off.

"I'll fucking kill them all, Kilsen," Allcot said, his body vibrating with agitation.

"Not if we kill you first," a muffled voice sounded from somewhere overhead.

Both of our heads snapped up, searching for the voice. I spotted the tiny speaker mounted in the corner just as Allcot let out a growl that ricocheted off the walls. I ran out into the hallway, quickly checking each of the rooms for whoever appeared to be listening in on us, but found no one.

Allcot was right, they'd set us up and were likely watching us from somewhere nearby. But the bayou was vast and had many remote areas. They could be just about anywhere, and finding them wouldn't be easy. I walked back into the far bedroom and found Allcot carefully removing Pandora's outfit from the wall. Her stilettos were at his feet along with the diamond pendant she normally wore. The one Nicola had likely used as a catalyst for her tracing spell since the pair of them wore matching pendants. Son of a bitch. That was going to make this a fuck ton harder.

"Goodbye, vampire," the ominous voice boomed. "It's too bad you brought the witch. We could've used her for our cause. But we all know how sacrifices have to be made. May you once again be reunited with your soul as you rest in peace."

I tightened my fingers around the hilt of my dagger and shifted into a fighting stance, more than ready to kick some ass. But instead of an army of paranormals coming after us like I'd expected, the door slammed shut and out of nowhere fire started to climb the walls.

A spell had been activated, likely by the distinct wording of the message Pandora's kidnapper had conveyed over the speaker.

Allcot didn't hesitate. He instantly turned toward the large bay window, grabbed an armchair, and swung. The legs of the chair broke clean off the frame, but the window miraculously stayed intact. The blow didn't even produce a crack.

"What the fuck?" Allcot stared at the sheared legs for just moment even as the smoke turned thick in the room. The fire was spreading quickly, and we were going to be crispy fried in a matter of minutes. Fire wasn't something a vampire could survive.

I coughed and ducked down under the rising smoke. "The windows have been spelled. They aren't going to budge unless I can break the curse."

Allcot let out a roar and swung again, this time putting the entire weight of his body behind the motion. He bounced off and came perilously close to the fire.

"Allcot!" I cried. "Move!"

He quickly scrambled back to my side, his eyes red and his fangs bared. "What are you waiting for, break the damned curse."

"Gladly. Just keep your ass away from the flames." I climbed to my feet, closed my eyes, and concentrated with everything I had. "Power of my blood, blood of my veins, I call up my strength and command thy will." Magic rushed through my limbs, my hands lighting up with blue light. "Power of my blood, blood of my veins, cut through the binds, let us cross the line."

"Kilsen, now!" Allcot demanded.

I rushed toward the floor-to-ceiling windows, my dagger raised, and let out a cry of determination as my dagger pierced the magical barrier. The glass shattered right along with the spell. Suddenly there was nothing to stop my forward motion, and I sailed headfirst through the third-story window.

Time seemed to slow down as visions of Willow, Talisen, and even Link flashed in my mind, followed closely by an image of Dax smiling down at me. The surge of pure emotion called up a swell of magic, but it wasn't focused and I had no way to channel my power to cushion my fall. My magic didn't work that way. The best I could hope for was a landing on the grass where I could tuck and roll.

Unfortunately, the gravel was coming fast. Acting on instinct, I spun my body in the air, made sure my feet were aiming for the earth, and did my best to remain relaxed. Once I hit the ground, my best option was to tuck and roll after the initial impact. It would hurt like a bitch, but I'd be damned if I was going to die today.

Barking filled the spring air, and before the ground rushed up to meet me, strong hands grabbed me and we shot up in the air, hovered for a moment, then slowly came back down to earth.

Allcot. He'd caught me.

"Thanks," I said as he let me go and the two of us stood there, staring at the inferno blazing before us.

"I think maybe I'm the one who should be thanking you," he said. "Fire isn't my favorite element."

I snorted out a humorless laugh. "I'd say that's an understatement."

"Perhaps. I owe you one, Kilsen." He turned and stalked back over to the car.

I glanced down at Link. He was pacing in front of me, still in wolf form. I placed a hand on the top of his head, soothing him. "Let's go, Link. Looks like our chances of finding any clues just went up in smoke."

My boots crunched on the gravel as I made my way to the car where Allcot was waiting. But Link didn't follow. Instead, he ran over to the side of the house and barked once.

"What is it, boy?" I asked him, squinting through the billowing smoke.

He barked again, and this time he ran flat out, disappearing into the haze.

I glanced at Allcot. "Looks like the wolf's found something."

Chapter Thirteen

*A*llcot's eyes blazed with fury as he followed Link, his movements sleek and graceful and just as predatory as a cheetah. I ran to catch up with him and the wolf, my eyes stinging from the smoke-filled air.

Moving deeper into the smoke, I pulled my T-shirt up over my mouth and put my head down. The heat from the burning house prickled my skin, setting me on edge. Whatever Link had found had better be worth it, I thought. Because if we survived the premeditated attack and the fall from the third story of the house just to get swallowed up in blaze anyway, I was going to be supremely pissed.

"Kilsen, get over here," Allcot ordered.

I followed the sound of his voice, my eyes too watery to see much of anything. But then the wind shifted directions, taking the smoke with it. I took a deep breath, blinking rapidly, and my vision cleared. My eyes widened as I stared at the vampire nailed to a shed. He was held up by a total of five lawn stakes, one in each of his hands, one through his sternum, and one each through his ankles.

"Holy shit."

Allcot snarled at the vampire, his fangs bared.

I'd never seen the leader of the Cryrique look so savage, so feral, before. The cool, cold-as-ice persona I'd come to know so well had vanished. There was nothing left of the CEO businessman, only a pissed-off vampire who'd given in to the beast inside himself.

"Where is she?" Allcot demanded, lashing one hand out and grabbing the other vampire by the throat.

The redheaded vampire looked almost identical to Carter Voelkel, only his face was slightly rounded with a few more age lines. There was no doubt the two were related. It was impossible to tell how long he'd been staked to the shed, but it'd been long enough. The wounds around each of the stakes had already healed. Curiously, he still had a bloody wound on his face.

The vampire didn't even try to speak as hatred swam in his blue gaze.

"Eadric, you're going to have to let go if we want to get answers," I said conversationally.

Allcot only squeezed the other vamp's neck harder.

The redheaded vamp's eyes bulged and a bone cracked under the weight of Allcot's fist.

"Are you trying to break his neck?" I asked the Cryrique leader.

"Yes," he said, "I'd like nothing better than to rip his head off."

"That would be productive," I said sarcastically. "I seriously doubt we're going to get another potential witness just handed to us, but if you feel that strongly, then maybe you should just end him. Put him out of his misery and we'll go about our business, trying to find someone else with answers." I had no idea why Allcot hated the other vampire, but in that moment I didn't care. Whatever it was, we had more important matters to deal with.

Allcot turned his steely glare on me and hissed.

I raised my hands, palms up, and shrugged as if the next move was entirely up to him. It wasn't. If Allcot attempted to kill the vampire before we questioned him, I wouldn't hesitate to stake him with my dagger... the cursed one that would knock his ass out. "What do you say, Allcot? Should we find out what he knows before ending him?"

There was a long, pregnant pause.

I tapped my finger on the hilt of my blade and waited.

"Fine," Allcot said with a sneer. He leaned into the other vamp and said, "Move one muscle and my companion here will turn your ass to ash, got it?"

"I will?" I asked before I could stop myself.

"Yes, you will," Allcot snapped as he released his hold on the other vampire. "Keep your dagger ready."

"Oh, right." I took a step forward and held the dagger up, pointing the tip straight at his heart. "Ever seen one of these before, carrot top? The magic in the blade makes it feel like your insides are on fire."

"Don't fucking call me that," he rasped.

"Then what should I call you?"

"Dante."

"Seriously?" I said, shaking my head. "Is that your given name, or did you just decide Dante made you sound cool?"

The vampire averted his gaze, not meeting my eyes, and let out a barely audible huff of annoyance.

"Oh gods. It's not your real name." I shook my head in

pity. "Listen, Dante. I'm not sure anyone's ever told you this, but picking a cooler name doesn't do anything to help with your cool points. In fact, I'd say it's probably a strike against you. It says you know you're uncool and are trying too hard. If I were you, I'd have gone with something more like Rusty or Smoke or even Coal. But Dante? Come on. No one's buying that."

Allcot let out a snort of amusement, and I was glad I'd managed to distract him from his single-minded determination to annihilate the vamp.

"Shut the fuck up, Kilsen," Dante said, glaring at me now.

"Oh, you know who I am. That's interesting. But I think we'll save that story for later." I inched closer, tightening my grip on the dagger. "For now, let's start with who did this to you?"

He ignored me.

"If you cooperate, we might help you down, but—"

"No you won't." He nodded his head toward Allcot. "He won't let you."

"Seems you're not as stupid as you look," Allcot said.

I glanced between them. "You two know each other?"

"You could say that." Allcot nudged me out of the way, stepped up to the vampire, and pressed a sharpened fingernail to Dante's neck. A thin line of blood beaded from the shallow scrape. "Why don't you tell Kilsen here exactly who you are, Dante?"

He scowled and shook his head.

"No? I guess it's up to me then." Allcot took a step back and, in a flat, expressionless tone said, "He's Pandora's ex, and I'd bet money she's the one who nailed his ass to this shed."

"Pandora's ex?" I asked, shocked. Eadric and Pandora were like an institution. It had never crossed my mind that there was a time when they hadn't been together. Of course, that was faulty logic as everyone had pasts and history. "But how come you think Pandora did this to him? How could she have done that if she's captured?"

Allcot moved in close again, grabbed the vampire's jaw and jerked his head to the side.

The vampire let out a grunt.

"See this?" Allcot ran his thumb over the one remaining bloody mark on the vampire's skin. "See how it hasn't healed?"

"Yeah." I squinted, trying to make out the shape of the wound. "Is that a fleur-de-lis?"

"Yes. Now ask me who's been working on a line of cursed rings that are designed to be used during an attack and have the added benefit of magically scarring the attacker."

"Nicola?" I guessed, impressed at her ingenuity.

"And guess who has been testing them out for her?"

"Pandora."

"Right again, Kilsen," Allcot said, slamming Dante's head against the wall. "This mark right here proves they've been fighting within the past couple of hours. Because while the curse leaves a mark, it does heal enough to just leave a scar." He tugged his sleeve up and showed me his inner arm. An identical mark was just below the crook of his elbow, only Allcot's had turned into a pink scar and was no longer a fresh wound. "I'd say Dante's here will look just like this within a few hours."

"Holy shit. That means Pandora was here *recently*." I turned and scanned the area, already knowing she couldn't be anywhere near. If she were, Link would've scented her.

Those fresh tire tracks in the mud guaranteed she'd either driven off by herself or had been recaptured and hauled away again. It was hard to say which scenario was most likely.

"She was and Dante here likely knows where they're taking her next, don't you, Dante?"

I frowned. "Why would anyone leave him behind with information they clearly wouldn't want you to have?"

"Insurance," Allcot said, his cold, sinister smile sending a chill up my spine despite the warm, humid day. "Just in case their trap didn't work. They left me a gift so I'll be sure to show up again for the next round of cat and mouse."

I glanced back and forth between Dante and Allcot, my skin prickling from their mutual hatred as I tried to make sense of what Allcot was telling me.

"You really pissed someone off, didn't you, Dante?" Allcot tsked. "Looks like whoever you're working with wants you dead."

They must, otherwise they'd never have left him here for Allcot to find.

"Did they finally figure out your loyalty is shit? What did you do? Try to sell Pandora to the highest bidder?"

Dante's lips twisted into a maniacal grin. "That bitch is worth a lot of money."

Allcot's precarious hold on his control snapped, and he grabbed the vampire, yanking him clear off the structure.

Dante let out a piercing cry as his flesh tore open once again from the lawn stakes that had been holding him up. Allcot threw him back against the shed, causing the entire thing to collapse around the other vampire.

"Shit," I muttered, taking a step back to stay out of the fray. I didn't personally care if Allcot beat him to a pulp. Clearly Dante was a worthless member of vampire society.

But I did care if Allcot killed him before we got more answers.

Allcot reached into the rubble and grabbed Dante with one hand, his other fist already sailing toward Dante's face. But Dante came out of the rubble with a broken two-by-four in his grasp, and before Allcot's fist connected, Dante rammed the jagged piece into Allcot's shoulder, tearing the flesh open and knocking Allcot off-balance.

Dante took his opening and flew at Allcot, his fangs bared.

Allcot spun, but he wasn't fast enough and Dante's fangs sank right into Allcot's neck. Still on their feet, they were a tangle of limbs and fangs and grunts.

Calmly, I walked right up to the grappling vampires and said, "Enough! Eadric, control yourself. We have work to do —Pandora, Willow, and Talisen are still missing, remember?"

Neither acknowledged my reasoning, not that I'd expected them to, but it'd been worth a shot.

"You realize you leave me no choice, right?" Again, nothing. "Okay then."

I reached for my other blade and waited for my opening, then lunged. The weapon slid easily into Dante's back and he froze.

Startled, Allcot froze too. Then his eyes found my blade and he started to laugh. He stepped away from the incapacitated vampire and nodded at me. "Well played, Kilsen."

"Bitch," Dante said, not daring to move a muscle.

"Call me that again, vampire, and I'll twist this knife." I pushed it in deeper, just to make my point. "It won't likely kill you since I didn't use the cursed one... this time, but it's hard to say. Depends on how close it is to your heart."

He let out a snarl. "What do you want from me?"

I leaned in and in a harsh whisper, I said, "I want to know everything. Who has Pandora, why they're toying with Allcot, and where the hell are Willow Rhoswen and Talisen Kavanagh?"

Chapter Fourteen

"*I* don't fucking know," Dante said through clenched teeth.

"He knows," Allcot said, sounding bored. "He's just run out of bargaining chips."

I glanced back at Allcot, who'd untangled himself from the other vampire. He and Link were flanking me on either side, both of them ready to spring into action if Dante tried to get the best of me. I smiled, acknowledging their presence.

Then I held my cursed blade up to the vampire's neck. "Answer me, or I'll shove this down your throat. And trust me when I say it will hurt worse than the fires of hell."

He grunted, clearly not believing me. I sliced the blade along his cheek. A scream tore from him as he jerked forward, taking me with him. My blade sank deeper and he froze again.

"Told you to trust me that this shit would hurt. Now, answers."

"Fuck you."

"Maybe another time," I said sweetly and lifted my blade to his face again.

The vampire sucked in a sharp breath. "All right! I'll tell you what I know."

"This better be good or else I think you'll find yourself roasting in the fire still smoldering behind us."

"Dammit. I don't know everything. But unless I get some assurance you're not going to waste me, I'm not going to tell you anything."

The fear in his voice was enough to convince me he'd spill whatever he'd learned. Or at least enough that it'd give us another path to follow. "All right. If you tell us everything you know, I promise to let you walk away."

"And what about your henchmen back there? Will you control the wolf and the vampire?"

"The wolf yes. Allcot? No one controls him."

"Allcot?" Dante said. "Deal?"

"Deal. But if I find out Pandora's already dead, I'll tear your head right off."

The vampire in front of me shuddered, and I suddenly knew what it meant to put the fear of God into someone. Or at least the fear of Eadric Allcot. Curiously, I'd never been all that afraid of the Cryrique leader, but then I'd never double-crossed him or harmed his consort either.

"Allcot is right. I was going to sell Pandora," Dante said. Allcot hissed again and Dante rushed to add, "Sell to the Cryrique. I released her and was going to offer her up in return for a wad of cash. You'd pay a lot to have your woman back, wouldn't you, Allcot?"

"I don't respond well to extortion," Allcot said, circling us as he glared at Dante. "And don't lie to me. I know your brother would've never forgiven such a betrayal."

"I swear on my tortured soul!" he cried, holding his hands partially up in surrender. "I only took this job because my brother said they'd pay off my debts."

"Debts?" I asked.

"Gambling. Women. Bad business deals. The usual," he said. "Nothing like this shit. I didn't sign up for this. And I certainly didn't know they were going to abduct Pandora. For fuck's sake. If anyone knows how crazy that bitch is, it's me."

"She does have a certain flair for the dramatic," Allcot said, puffing his chest out, a look of pride flashing over his face.

"Yes, we all know Pandora is your perfect match in every way," I said, rolling my eyes at Allcot. "Can we move on?"

"You know, Kilsen," Allcot said, his gaze sweeping over me. "If anyone ever turned you vampire, you'd be just like her."

I ignored his remark, refusing to even entertain the idea of becoming a vamp. "So you freed Pandora," I said to Dante. "What happened after that?"

"I got her outside, but the shifters were waiting for me and—"

"Shifters?" I asked. "Which shifters? Which pack?"

"No idea. Rogue shifters, I think. If they were with a pack, I don't know which one. They never talked about it."

"Fuck." My gaze met Allcot's, and his superior expression had "I told you so" written all over it. "Okay, so the shifters were there. Then what?"

"Pandora went insane. She accused me of lying to her, that I only told her I'd take her back to Allcot to get her to cooperate. That's when she attacked half the shifters. She took out two of them before I grabbed her, trying to get her away from them. There too many to fight off. I figured we'd make a break for it. Fly away from here, but she tried to take off without me. If I'd let that happen, those shifters would've killed me on the spot for betraying them."

"So you stopped her from leaving?" I asked. "Because if she got away, there'd be no reason for Allcot to pay your ransom money, right?"

"That too," he said, hanging his head. "And when I grabbed her, demanding she take me with her, she went into a rage, grabbed the garden stakes that were on the porch, and nailed me to the shed. Told me I could rot there forever as far as she was concerned."

"So why didn't she leave after that?" I asked, knowing damned well she possessed the same ability to fly that Allcot did.

"They tranq'd her."

Shocked rattled me. "Vampire tranquilizer? How did they get their hands on it? It's highly controlled."

"Don't be naïve, Kilsen," Allcot hissed. "Everyone has a price."

I stared at him. "You're not implying the director—"

"No, not necessarily. But it's not out of the realm of possibility. Besides, she's not the only one who has access to the drug, now is she?" He lowered his gaze to my feet where I did indeed have a tranq gun strapped to my ankle.

"No tracker would sell that. It's too dangerous." But even as I said the words, I knew my statement was a lie. Power and money ruled New Orleans, and no one was above corruption. In fact, there was a reason there was only a handful of people I trusted. Willow, Tal, and Dax. The others, like Allcot—we had a mutual understanding, but neither of us fully trusted the other. I shook my head and frowned. "Point taken," I said to Allcot, and then turned my attention back to Dante. "Where did they get it?"

"Fuck if I know. That's above my pay grade."

"Fine. Where did they tell you they were going next?" I asked.

"They said they were taking up residence on the ghost ship at Poland Wharf. Tomorrow night."

"Tomorrow night?" I asked, my mind reeling. It was a setup. The perfect con. If Allcot and I were off "saving" Pandora, we'd be out of the way for Asier.

"Yes. I don't know where they'll be before then."

"I don't believe you for one second, Dante," I said, pressing the dagger to his throat. "I know exactly what's supposed to happen tomorrow night, and it has nothing to do with Pandora."

He flinched, and I knew I'd hit a nerve.

"Tell me where they're taking Pandora. Is it the same place where Willow and Talisen are?"

"I don't know! I don't know, I swear!" he cried.

Allcot strolled around to face Dante. "You have five seconds to tell me where we can find Pandora, or I'm going to end you. Got it?"

Dante let out a whimper. "They'll kill me."

"They won't have a chance," I said. "Because at this point, I'm ready to let Allcot have his way."

"Jesus," he said, hanging his head. "I honestly don't know. And I do think they're planning on taking Pandora to that ghost ship."

"Dante," I said, "this blade is gonna do some real damage here in a second."

"I-I have a couple of guesses. Solid ones."

"Spit them out," Allcot said.

"They have a compound in English Turn. It used to belong to Bazil Baker, that famous singer turned vampire. He disappeared a few years ago and left it to his nephew. I heard the crew talking about crashing there."

"I know it," Allcot said.

Of course he did. He knew just about every rich, powerful, or famous person who ever set foot in the city.

"Where else? And just give it to us straight, I'm tired of this game," I said.

"Oak Street. The peacock-blue house just before River Road."

"And Willow and Tal? Where are they?"

He shook his head. "I don't know anything about where they are. I was only hired to keep Pandora in line."

"Will your brother Carter know?" I asked, my gut telling me Carter Voelkel was one of the main orchestrators of this entire ordeal.

"Yes, but you won't find him," Dante said as he glanced back at me. "He only shows his face when he's putting a plan in action. Now that the wheels are in motion, he'll be back in hiding."

Dante's words confirmed my suspicions. The vampire and shifters had been working together. Carter had distracted me while the shifters took Pandora. But what exactly had they wanted her for? Realization dawned on me.

Pandora was the distraction.

They needed to take her to distract Allcot while they completed the ritual, using a fae under his protection—the one and only accessible fairy with any notable power in the city.

"How do you get in touch with your brother?" I asked.

"I don't. He gets in touch with me."

"How?"

"He calls me or comes by my house. Why? You want me to give him a message?"

"No." Keeping my cursed blade against his throat, I used my other hand to reach into his pocket and pull out his phone. "I'm going to keep this. And if you turn it off between now and tomorrow night, I'll hunt you down and end you, got it?"

He nodded. "Yeah. Got it."

I glanced at Allcot. "Anything else?"

Allcot took two steps, standing only inches from the other vampire. His eyes blazed with pure hatred. "If I ever catch you near Pandora again, you'll wish I'd let Kilsen here stick that cursed dagger down your throat. Understand?"

"Yeah, man. I get it. But Allcot, about that money——"

"Shut him up," Allcot ordered as he turned and headed back by the smoldering house.

"You're really fucking stupid," I said.

The vampire didn't say a word. He just hung his head, dejected.

"I do have two more questions before I take this knife out of your back."

"I don't know anything else," he said defiantly.

"I doubt that. First, what is Pandora wearing now that they stripped her of her gala outfit?"

His head popped up and he glanced back at me, incredulous. "That's what you want to know?"

"Yes. Is she dressed, or did you bastards make her run around in her lace underwear?"

His eyes glazed over as he took in my words, but he shook his head. "She was wearing an oversized T-shirt. No shoes."

I shook my head, annoyed. At least she wasn't naked. "Do

you know or have you ever heard of anyone by the name of Blazer or Seth?"

"Blazer? Yeah, I know a Blazer. Cool guy. Good with computers."

"You've seen Blazer?" I asked, my voice rising in excitement. "When? Where?"

"Whoa. Clam down, witch. It's been a few years. He helped Carter hack into some corporation's system. Then he disappeared. Too bad, 'cause I could use some of his help right about now. Just a little transfer of money and I'd be in the clear."

"*Two* years ago? You're completely sure about that?" How was that possible? My brother had been missing for eight.

"Positive."

"If you're lying, I'll end you."

"I'm not lying! Jesus, lady. What do you want with him anyway?"

"Never mind." I wasn't going to trust my secrets to the enemy, and he'd already indicated Seth had disappeared. There was nothing left to discuss. I dropped the cursed dagger from his neck, yanked the blade out of his back, and shoved him forward with a knee. "Go on. Get out of here before Allcot changes his mind."

The vampire swore as he stumbled, but when he found his balance, he pressed his hand to the marks on his neck and eyed me. "If you find him, tell him I have work for him."

"Huh?" I asked, distracted, running through all the places Seth might stay when he was in the city. A safe house made the most sense. But why wouldn't he contact me? Had he been deep undercover at the Void all this time? Was that why they'd pretended he'd gone missing? If so, they'd even gone through the trouble to doctor his Void records. I gritted my teeth in frustration, knowing for certain that anything was possible. If there was any truth at all to the vampire's claim, as soon as Willow and Tal were safe, I'd make it my sole mission to find him.

"Christ, Kilsen," Allcot said from out of nowhere. "You looking to get yourself killed?"

I jumped, startled out of my thoughts. "What?"

"You're just standing there, staring off at nothing. If you hadn't done such a good job scaring the shit out of that jackass Dante, he could've taken you without even breaking a sweat. What are you doing?"

"Thinking," I said, realizing Dante had fled while I was lost in thought. "Need to plan our next move."

"I'm already on it. Time to take a trip to English Turn."

Chapter Fifteen

$\mathcal{D}$ax sat, drumming his fingers on his leg as he impatiently waited outside Bandu's private office. The leader of the pack had been holed up on the phone for over an hour, and Dax had just about lost patience. He stood and started to pace, his inner wolf antsy.

"You should go for a run, man."

Dax jerked his head up and nodded to Leo. The young shifter had just appeared from the adjoining kitchen and was leaning against the doorframe. He had an apple in one hand and a hunk of jerky in the other.

"Maybe later," Dax said. "How was the rest of the search? Any leads?"

Leo shook his head. "Nope. It's strange too. I don't think we've ever been out canvassing before when we didn't run into some bullshit revolving around the vampires. Even in the daylight, there's always chatter about the night before or a daywalker causing trouble. It's like we're in the eye of the storm."

"Or the calm before the storm," Dax said, his fingers itching to text Phoebe. He hated the way they'd left things back at the safe house. He wanted to discuss his sudden promotion within the pack, wanted to ask her about the notebook and Seth Kilsen. It hadn't escaped his notice that the man shared her last name. What was he to her? A brother? Cousin? Husband?

He shook his head. No. Not husband. She would've told him, right?

"Dude, relax. You look like you're going to come right out of your skin." The young shifter gave Dax a lopsided grin. "What is it? Woman problems?"

Dax stretched his neck but didn't answer.

Leo laughed. "It *is* woman problems. Well, in that case, a run is definitely in order. Your head will be clearer after you blow off some steam."

"I can't. I need to talk to Bandu." He needed to find out what the leader knew about Carter Voelkel and Asier. As far as Dax was concerned, the redheaded vampire was at the center of the abductions. If he could find him, he'd have a lead.

Leo brushed his shaggy hair out of his eyes and frowned. "Is that what you're doing in here?"

Dax nodded. "It's important. So thanks, but—"

"Dax, Bandu left twenty minutes ago. He said you were in charge until he gets back."

"You're kidding me." Dax turned abruptly and knocked on Bandu's office door. When no one answered, he cracked the door open and peeked in. Sure enough, the office was empty. He strode in and glanced around. "What the fuck? I was sitting here the entire time waiting for him."

Leo, who'd followed him into the office, shrugged. "Maybe he was just messing with you?"

Or maybe he didn't want Dax to know he'd left. An uneasy feeling coiled in Dax's gut. Something wasn't right. Ever since Bandu had made Dax his second, he'd been holed up and unavailable, almost as if he was avoiding his new beta.

Dax walked over to the desk, scanned the stack of paperwork separated into three piles. More victims. At least these weren't dead. But they did all have something in common—each one was an allegation against the Cryrique for feeding on humans without consent. Another sheet of paper sat off to the side. Dax picked it up and felt a wave of relief wash over him when he realized it was a formal complaint to be lodged with the city against Allcot and his vampires. Dax had been worried that since the shifters had appointed themselves protectors of the city that they'd start to take matters into their own hands. The complaint proved Bandu was still following protocol.

"This looks promising," Dax said.

"What does?" Leo asked, moving to look over Dax's shoulder.

"Oh, that." He made a disgusted face. "The city won't do anything. Bandu just files those to prove a point. No one ever takes action."

Dax frowned. "They don't? You sure? They're supposed to forward them to the Arcane."

Leo shook his head. "Nope. They only forward the worst ones. These? The victims usually see a healer and then can barely remember what happened. And because they don't make waves, the city ignores them, pretends the problem isn't that bad. Bandu says it's because the city wants to keep the Cryrique happy. Likes the millions in tax revenue they generate every year."

That niggling feeling that something was off flared to life again as Dax listened to Leo. His explanation wasn't what Dax had experienced while working for the Void. The investigative agency had people in city government who were extremely vigilant about paranormal complaints, transferring all but the most minor ones to the Void. As far as Dax knew, actual vampire attacks on humans were down significantly.

Was he wrong about that? Was there a massive, city-wide government cover-up that had caused Bandu and the pack to turn into a watchdog group? That was entirely possible. Dax picked up one of the reports on the desk and read the complaint. Twenty-two-year-old woman, recent college graduate, worked at the Red Door.

The Red Door? That was Allcot's place down on Frenchmen Street. Very few humans worked there, and the ones who did were trusted members of the inner circle, usually waiting to be turned. It wasn't easy for a human to get a job there. Dax moved on to the complaint.

Lacy Wallace claims she worked at the Red Door for thirteen months. During that time, she was continually pressured to seek vampirism. When it became clear Miss Wallace had no interest in turning vampire, her direct supervisor, Bella Jaxon, attacked her and fed from her until Miss Wallace passed out. She was fired two days later and told she was let go due to her refusal to turn vampire.

Dax frowned and picked up the other two complaints. The stories were similar except the women worked at the corporate offices, but they also each accused their direct supervisors. The Cryrique did employ plenty of humans in their offices. They had to in order to keep the organization running. There weren't enough vampires to sustain such a force.

But the clubs? That was a different story. And Lacy Wallace didn't pass the smell test. At least not with Dax. He knew Bella Jaxon, and to his knowledge she'd only turned two vampires in her years, and both of them were her flesh-and-blood sisters.

All of Allcot's vampires were extremely selective in who they chose to become part of the hive. The act of turning a vampire was highly personal and intimate, and not a venture vampires took lightly. When a newbie was turned, the vampire who brought them over was then responsible for the fledgling in every way, emotionally, physically, financially. Unless Lacy Wallace had some sort of close relationship with Bella, it was hard to imagine she'd have been pressured to turn. It just wasn't Bella's or the other Cryrique vampires' modus operandi.

"Leo," Dax said, "do you have plans this afternoon?"

"No. I was going to do more canvassing with Dali, but he's out getting food with his girl. Why?"

"I want to check something out. I could use backup." It was never a good idea to go into vampire territory without a partner, and while Leo wasn't his first choice, he was a good fighter. He'd do if things got out of hand for some reason.

The younger shifter's eyes gleamed with excitement. "You mean something for the Arcane?"

Dax paused for a moment, wondering how to answer. Was this for the Arcane? He didn't exactly know. But he just couldn't shake his gut feeling that the complaints were bogus. And if they were, he needed to get to the bottom of why.

"Yeah. But unofficial for the moment. Just following up on a hunch."

"Absolutely! Let me just text Dali."

"No." Dax shook his head. "Let's keep this quiet for now. At least until we know if we have anything worth talking about.

"Okay, sure. Yeah. I can do that. Should I arm myself?" The excitement in the kid's eyes only fed Dax's unease. He was far too willing to do whatever Dax asked of him just to get a taste of the action.

"No, kid. Not this time. Where we're going, you'll be lucky if they even let you in the door. If they find out you're armed, you'll never make it past the bouncer."

"Oh." His excitement vanished, and he shoved his hands in his pockets. "Okay, but where exactly are we going?"

"You'll see."

"Marrok. What the hell are you doing here?" Branson, the bouncer at the Red Door asked. "I thought you were out with Kilsen, hunting down Pandora and those two fae."

"Kilsen is with Allcot," Dax said, as if that in any way explained why he was at the club at four in the afternoon. He and Leo were just inside the entrance of the club in a small holding area, waiting to see if Branson was going to let them through the security check.

"I see. That's too bad for you," he said with a sleazy leer. "You know Allcot's always had a thing for that hot piece of ass, right?"

A growl rumbled from Dax's throat.

The tall bouncer threw his head back and laughed. "I knew you had a thing for her. Poor bastard."

"Phoebe's hot," Leo said from behind Dax. "But Dax doesn't have anything to worry about. She'd never let a vampire get his fangs into her. She doesn't swing that way."

Branson sneered at Leo. "Who the fuck is this?"

"He's my shadow for the day. Considering a career with the Arcane," Dax said offhandedly. "Which brings me to why we're here. I need to talk to Bella Jaxon. Is she around?"

"Bella? What do you want to talk to her for?"

"Just need to ask her some questions. I'm trying to corroborate a story," Dax said, doing his best to not raise the bouncer's suspicions. If he thought Bella was in any kind of trouble, Dax would never get through those doors. "Nothing to worry about."

The bouncer shook his head, a look of disgust on his face. "This is what you're doing while those two fae are missing? I thought they were friends of yours, man. Jesus." He laughed. "And they say vampires are coldhearted."

Dax didn't take the bait. He just stood there, waiting.

"Whatever." Branson waved a hand. "Talk to Bella if you want, but I'd be careful if I were you. She's pissed as hell about Pandora, and I don't know how she's going to take talking to a couple of mutts."

"What did you say, bloodsucker?" Leo spat out from behind Dax.

Branson glared at the kid then shifted his dangerous gaze back to Dax. "Control your pup, or I'll do it for you."

Leo stepped around Dax, his fists clenched and muscles straining as he got in Branson's face. "Bring it on, asshole. I'll rip you—"

"Enough." Dax grabbed Leo by his shirt collar and hauled him back before Branson took it upon himself to break the kid's neck.

"Hey!" Leo flailed, trying to squirm out of Dax's hold. "Let me go. I can't let that vamp get away with speaking to me like that. Did you hear what he said? He called me a fucking mutt! That piece of——"

"I said enough!" Dax roared as he slammed Leo up against the wall, holding him in place. "Didn't you hear me, Leo? You will control yourself, or this is the last time you'll ride with me, got it?"

"Fuck, Dax. Let me down. I thought we were pack. I thought we——"

Dax leaned in close, pressing his forearm against the young shifter's throat. Then he lowered his voice and in a harsh whisper said, "We're in vampire territory. Do you understand that?"

Leo didn't move, just stared at Dax, his eyes wide.

"I *said* do you understand that?"

"Yeah," he croaked out.

"That means we play by their rules. If you want inside their private club, then if they want to insult you, they can and will. It's their way of getting under your skin and rattling you."

"It's bullshit," Leo rasped.

"So fucking what? They have something we want. We can either put up with it or not. But if we choose not, it just means we'll leave empty-handed. So for today, what do you think we're going to do?"

Leo closed his eyes, looking pained.

"That's right, kid. We're going to take it, because we don't have a choice. If you want to throw down with Branson when you meet him out on the streets, then be my guest. But for today, if you're with me, you'll take his bullshit and swallow it until we get what we came for. Tuck your ego and pride away, son. Neither will help you in this game. Understand me?"

Leo opened his pale blue eyes and opened his mouth, but no sound came out. Dax pulled his arm away and raised his eyebrows in a question. Leo cleared his throat and said, "I understand."

"Good." Dax released the shifter and smoothed his shirt. "Now we can get back to business." He turned back to Branson. "I apologize for my apprentice. He hasn't quite learned his place in this world yet."

Branson eyed Leo. "Why should I let you in my club after that outburst?"

Leo stared at the bouncer for a moment then shifted his gaze to Dax.

"He probably wants an apology," Dax said with an amused half smile.

"Yeah. An apology would be nice. And a twenty. I want to take my girl somewhere nice after work," Branson said.

"With just a twenty?" Dax scoffed. "What are you gonna do, take her to the park and open up a box or two of wine?"

"Marrok is right," Branson said with a nod. "Better make it a fifty."

"Fuck," Leo said, grimacing.

"Expensive lesson, kid," Dax said.

"No fucking kidding." Leo dug in his pocket and came up with thirty-two dollars. He held the bills out to Branson. "It's all I got. Take it or leave it."

"I'll take it." Branson turned to Dax and grinned.

"Thanks, Marrok. Now I can upgrade to something with a cork."

"Good for you, dude." Dax glanced over his shoulder. "Come on, Leo. And keep your temper in check. You can't afford to piss off another vamp."

Leo shoved his hands into his pockets and hunched his shoulders, looking every bit like a sullen teenager.

Chapter Sixteen

Once Dax and Leo passed through the security screening, they paused for a moment, letting their vision adjust to the dark interior. Being that it was a vampire club, there weren't any windows and the lights were adjusted for a soft glow.

Dax led the way across the room and nodded to the pretty redheaded vampire behind the bar. "Hey, Cassie. How's it going?"

"Not too bad. But it's early yet." She swept her gaze over him, her eyes lingering on his chest before moving lower. She eyed his crotch and licked her lips, purposely trying to torture him. It didn't work though. It never did. Vampires just weren't his type. "You're looking mighty fine today."

"Thanks." Dax smiley lazily at her, giving her the reaction he knew she was waiting for. "You're not looking too bad yourself."

"It's the eternal-youth thing," she said with a wink and turned her attention to Leo. "Now, what do we have here?"

"Cassie, this is Leo. He's a friend of mine. Leo, this is Cassie. She's the one who's really in charge around here. Right, Cassie?"

She chuckled. "That's right. This place would fall apart without me." She swept the same seductive gaze over Leo and leaned across the counter, giving him a perfect view of her cleavage. "I'd really like to be in charge of this one for the night. What do you say, Leo? Are you game?"

The younger shifter's gaze was locked on Cassie's ample bosom as he shook his head.

"No?" Cassie asked in a mock shy tone as she ran one fingernail lightly down his forearm. "But just think of the things I could teach you. A young pup like you, so full of vigor and energy... Damn, it would be one hell of an evening."

"Uh..." Leo swallowed thickly. "I um..."

Cassie threw her head back and laughed. "So young. What I wouldn't do to get my fangs into you, handsome."

Leo jerked back and shook his head, the seduction haze vanishing instantly. "No, thank you, ma'am. I'm not, um, available."

Cassie pushed her bottom lip out in a little pout. "That's too bad, Leo. I was looking for someone to make me purr."

"I bet you were," Dax said, rolling his eyes. "Give the kid a break, huh? We're actually here on business."

Cassie swept her gaze over Leo one more time and sighed. "Too bad. I like the green ones. They're easier to train."

"I'm not green," Leo said, clearly offended.

"Sure, kid." She smiled patiently at him. "If you say so." Then she turned to Dax, her sex kitten demeanor vanishing as she straightened and eyed him with suspicion. "You said you're here on business?"

"Yeah. I have questions about an incident."

She rolled her eyes. "Who doesn't?"

"So you admit that it's usual for complaints to be filed against the management here?" Leo asked, his self-righteousness on full display.

"Dammit, Leo," Dax said. "What did I tell you after the shitshow with Branson?"

"I—"

Dax growled. "Shut the fuck up. I've got this handled."

The kid grimaced and took a step back, apparently finally getting the message his arrogant sideshow wasn't welcome.

Cassie chuckled. "Got him on a short leash, don't you?"

Dax ignored her question and asked, "Did you know Lacy Wallace? College age, human, claims to have worked here?"

"Lacy? Sure." Cassie nodded. "Cute blonde. She was very into the vampire lifestyle. Poor thing was so clueless she even wore a vial of blood around her neck. Very Angelina Jolie."

"She's enthralled with vampires then? Some sort of vampire worship going on?" Dax pulled out a small notebook and flipped it open.

"Definitely. Girl wants to be a vamp so bad she can taste it. I'm pretty sure that's the only reason Bella hired her. Most humans who aren't into it don't last long here."

"What does that mean, 'don't last long?'" Leo asked.

Dax wasn't happy his protégé wasn't obeying orders, but it was a question he was going to ask himself, so he let it slide.

"They can't handle it and they quit," Cassie said, placing three shot glasses on the bar. "Vampires have their own code of conduct. We don't really play by the regular rules of society." Her lips curved back into that seductive smile. "We're much less repressed."

"So she was sexually harassed?" Leo asked.

"She? You mean Lacy?"

Leo nodded. "Yeah, Lacy."

Cassie laughed and poured amber liquid into each of the shot glasses in front of her. "Boy, please. If anyone was doing the harassing, it was Lacy herself. I told you, she was relentless. She tried everything from flirting and charming, to seducing to get a vamp to turn her ass. It was embarrassing, to be honest. Finally Bella had to fire her because the customers were complaining."

"Does Bella have documentation?" Dax asked. He believed Cassie. The vampire was a one hundred percent straight shooter. If she or anyone else had been pursuing or harassing Lacy, she would've just spit it out. Cassie was telling the truth when she said the vamps at the Red Door weren't repressed in any way. Sexual innuendo was a way of life for them. None of them ever tried to hide it. And that's why he fully believed that Lacy had been trying to get herself turned.

"I don't know. Why don't you ask her yourself?" Cassie jerked her head, indicating the vampire in question was behind them.

Dax turned and nodded at the gorgeous, dark-skinned vampire. She was striking with her perfect mahogany skin and dark hair so long it nearly reached her ass.

"Dax Marrok," she said with a genuine smile. "What brings you by this lazy afternoon? I would've thought for sure you'd be out with that witch of yours searching for the fae couple." Her expression darkened and she shook her head.

"It's a real tragedy what happened to them. And Pandora as well. Allcot is just beside himself."

"Is he here? Have you heard from him?" Dax asked, more out of curiosity about where Phoebe might be rather than the Cryrique leader.

"No, no. I'm sure we won't see him until he can bring Pandora home." The vampire's eyes moistened, and she blinked back real tears. It was a side of her Dax had never seen before. A welcome side. "I don't know what I'll do if anything happens to her. She's like a sister to me."

Leo's mouth dropped open, and a look of shock filtered over his face as he stared at the lovely vampire.

"Jesus," Cassie scoffed. "You'd think the pup had never seen a vamp cry before."

"I… I guess I haven't," Leo said. "I've never really spoken to one outside of an altercation."

Cassie rolled her eyes. "Figures. Don't you think you'd be better served working off that energy in bed rather than trying to kick some vamp's ass just because he's different than you?"

"That's not why I fight vampires," Leo said.

"So explain it to me," Cassie said, handing him one of the shots of whiskey and batting her eyelashes at him. Good God, Dax thought. Cassie was relentless. He was certain that if she was given enough time, she'd for sure have the young shifter in the sack by the end of the day and have him thinking it was his idea.

"Why don't you two discuss that while Bella and I have a chat," Dax said, pushing himself off the bar and moving to Bella's side.

"Oh, I'd be happy to," Cassie said with a grin.

"Um, Dax? I think… I think I should…" Leo stammered.

"You'll be fine. Just go easy on the booze." Dax flashed him a shit-eating grin and pressed his hand to the small of Bella's back as they walked down the hall and into her office.

"Have a seat," she said, waving to a pair of pale blue velvet armchairs.

Dax sat in one while she sat in the other. He turned to the vampire, a woman he'd come to respect over the past six months. She was a levelheaded, steady force who seemed to mostly keep her staff in line. And she'd come to trust Dax herself, often passing along intel on dirty vampires. Though Dax had to admit that none of them ever worked for Cryrique.

"How are you holding up, Bella?"

"As well as to be expected. You? How come you're here and not out hunting the vampires who took Rhoswen and her husband?" She blinked then sucked in a sharp breath. "Wait, you don't think Cryrique had anything to do with that, do you?"

"No, but if I find out they did, I'll rain hellfire down on y'all," he said conversationally.

"Rightly so."

Her conviction made him remember why he'd always liked her. "I'm here trying to work out a hunch."

"Interesting." She perched on the edge of her seat and leaned in closer. "How can I help?"

"First, I have to ask about Lacy Wallace. Do you remember her?"

"The human?" Bella asked, her eyebrows shooting up in surprise. "Yes, why?"

Dax tapped his fingers on his thigh. "She's filing a formal complaint against you."

"For what?" The look on Bella's face made it clear she had no idea what this was about.

"Says you repeatedly pressured her to turn vampire, and when she finally said no, you attacked her. Fed from her without permission."

Bella stood abruptly, her expression incredulous. "You're joking, right? *Lacy Wallace* said I pressured her to turn?"

"I'm not." Dax frowned. "Want to tell me what happened there?"

Bella let out a huff of irritation. "That little piece of work. Total trash is what she is. A trust fund baby who is obsessed with eternal youth. I wouldn't turn her even if she was on her death bed and it was her only chance of survival. That woman would be a nightmare as a vampire. If someone did turn her, I bet she'd be in the Arcane jail the first week for attacking someone. It's all she knows how to do."

"Whoa. No love lost there then," Dax said.

"None at all." Bella shook her head and sat back down. "When Eadric finds out she lodged a complaint, there's going to be hell to pay."

Dax sat up straighter, concerned with what that might mean. "How so? You do realize intimidation will only make this worse, right?"

Bella scoffed. "Not intimidation. She'll get slapped with a lawsuit. She was given a year's severance and signed a nondisclosure. And she only got that because she—" Bella raised her hands and made air quotes as she continued, "—'slipped and cut her arm' in the store room. Only problem was Cassie saw Lacy slice her arm herself. Lacy apparently thought she'd drive one of us crazy with the smell of her blood and was trying to manipulate us. Eadric got her a healer and put her on leave that night. She was let go a week later."

"And the severance was because... Why?" Dax asked.

"To get her to go away quietly. Guess that backfired." Bella shrugged. "Let her file her complaint. We have plenty against her from patrons complaining about her asking them to turn her or hook up with her after work."

"I see." Dax nodded, knowing in his gut Bella was telling the truth. "So I'm guessing you never fed from her either?"

She snorted out an incredulous laugh. "Me, feed on Lacy Wallace? I'd rather drink rat blood."

"That's what I thought." Dax scribbled a couple of notes, completely convinced the report was false. He just wondered if the other two were as well, and if so, was Bandu actively recruiting former employees to lodge bogus complaints to bolster support for his vigilante pack? He was leaning toward yes. "Okay. If the complaint makes it up the chain of command, I'll make sure whoever ends up with it gets my notes. Thanks, Bella."

"Sure." She smiled warmly at him. "But I still don't quite understand why you're here instead of out looking for your fae friends."

"I have a hunch that all of this is part of the bigger picture. That's all."

"You think Lacy Wallace is involved?" she asked, her expression dubious.

"No, not directly. I'm thinking someone is pulling her strings." Dax put the notebook down and met Bella's gaze. "And that brings me to my next question. Were you at the gala last night?"

"Sure. Everyone was."

"Okay, good," he said. "I know at least a few of the guests

149

saw Pandora's abduction or glimpsed it. Were you one of them?"

"Actually yes, I couldn't tell you who they were. They were wearing hoodies and had their faces covered, so I'm useless in that sense."

Dax flipped his notebook open to a blank page. "Tell me everything you saw."

"Before or after those vampires antagonized that poor boy out there?" She jerked her head, indicating the front of house.

"You saw that? How they baited Leo and Dali?"

"Sure. Then you jumped in and defused the situation. Kept them from giving their control over to their wolves. I was impressed."

"Did you recognize those vamps?"

"Nope. No idea who they were. Never seen them in here before, that's for sure. I can tell you this though; that kind of bullshit wouldn't fly in here. Not that we get many shifters besides your fine ass." She winked.

Dax let out a small chuckle. "Too much fang for most."

She nodded her agreement then turned serious. "Now those shifters that took Pandora? I know I recognized one of them from somewhere, but I can't put my finger on it. I've been racking my brain trying to figure it out, but dammit, the memory won't surface."

"What do you mean the shifters who took Pandora?" he asked, eyeing her carefully. Allcot had claimed the same thing, but Dax hadn't believed it. It might've had something to do with the fact the vampire leader had been trying to rip Dax's head off. But if Bella was saying the same thing, and he'd always known her as being forthright, then he'd have to give the information serious consideration.

"Exactly what I said. As far as I know, no one here actually saw the moment they managed to subdue her." She met Dax's gaze, her expressive eyes stone-cold serious. "Can you imagine the fight that must've gone down? Pandora's not someone I'd want to contend with when she's pissed off. She's crazier than Allcot."

"You've got that right." Dax had seen Pandora out of control exactly once—when the Crimson Valley pack had tried to abduct Allcot. She and Phoebe had tracked them down fairly easily. And while Phoebe had done her best to defuse the situation, Pandora had taken matters into her own hands and drained four shifters in the time it took Phoebe to fight off one. She was savage. "Now, how do you know shifters took her if you didn't see them snatch her?"

"Oh, yes, well, I was headed out to my car in the parking garage to retrieve my phone when an SUV nearly ran me over. Thanks to my quick reflexes, I was able to jump out of the way in time, but I got an up-close-and-personal look inside that car. Pandora was slumped against the far window, obviously tranq'd. And there were two wolves in the back seat in the process of shifting."

There it was. The proof that shifters had taken her. But why? And why had Phoebe been lured away and set up by a vampire? The idea that vampires and shifters were working together to abducted Willow and Talisen and Pandora was insane, wasn't it? Why would a vampire help the shifters abduct Pandora? And why would the shifters help anyone, let alone a vampire, abduct the fae?

Unless… *Asier.*

What was it Phoebe had said about it? A ritual to save supernatural souls. Had a group of shifters and vampires teamed up to form some sort of cult? It was a strong possibility. In normal situations, vampires and shifters just didn't work together on that level. But if they were cooperating for a common goal and they were crazy enough to believe that sacrificing a fairy would save their souls then they were stupid enough to trust one another.

"I just wish I could place that wolf. I know I've seen him somewhere before," Bella continued.

"Can you describe him to me?"

"Sure. Dark gray, one black-tipped ear, one white-tipped ear. Blue eyes and white on the end of his tail. Know him?"

Dax shook his head. He didn't know anyone with one white ear and one black one. "I'll keep an eye out though."

Bella patted his arm. "I know you will, Dax. You're decent like that." She got up and stretched her arms over her head. "Looks like it's time to get to work."

"Wait, one more question," Dax said, standing to look her in the eye. "Does the term Asier mean anything to you?"

Bella jerked back as if she'd been slapped. "Where did you hear that word?"

"I can't really say."

"Is it part of this investigation?"

Dax nodded. He'd already brought it up, so it wasn't as if he could deny it. But he didn't want to tell her what he knew, which admittedly, wasn't much.

Bella got up and walked over to her desk. She eyed the calendar off to the side and gasped. "It's tomorrow night."

"You know what is it then?" Dax asked.

"Yes," she said, her body tense and her expression haunted. "It's pure evil."

Chapter Seventeen

*D*ax walked out of Bella's office sick to his stomach. The vampire had filled him in on the ritual of Asier and what they could expect to find should no one stop it in time. Willow and Talisen would be virtually unidentifiable.

The fact that it appeared the events of the night before were a coordinated effort by both shifters and vampires, with Pandora being abducted by shifters and Willow and Tal by vampires, pretty much confirmed for Dax that a cult had indeed formed and the fae were in serious danger.

Carter Voelkel had shown up to lure Phoebe away from the gala and abducted Pandora to keep Allcot distracted. Did that mean the shifter-vampire altercation had been a setup too? It had been the perfect distraction right before the fae and Pandora had been taken.

"Fuck!" Dax said. They'd been played. All of them.

He strode over to the bar and let out another curse. Leo was sitting on the stool, his legs spread with Cassie standing between them. She had her hands in his hair while she kissed her way down his neck, her lips lingering over his pulse. The young shifter had his head tilted back and his eyes closed, a stupid-as-fuck grin on his face.

"Leo!" Dax snapped. "Remove the vampire from your neck before she fangs you."

His head snapped up and he slid his hands down to her hips, jerking her off him.

"Hey, baby," Cassie said, her lips in that perfect pout again. "We were just getting started."

"Cass, let it be. We're done here," Dax said and jerked his head, indicating Leo should follow him.

"Um, sorry," Leo said and hastily scrambled to catch up with Dax.

"No tip?" Cassie called after them.

Leo paused and glanced back, but Dax grabbed him by the elbow and dragged him out of the club.

"She's fucking with you, man," Dax said. "Do not pay her anything. She's not a whore."

"I wasn't going to," Leo said indignantly.

"Sure." Dax pushed open the front door and was surprised to find the sun had already set. He strode quickly to his Trooper and jumped in. As soon as Leo was in the passenger seat, he slammed the truck in gear and took off.

"Damn, what's the hurry, man?" Leo asked.

"We need to find Bandu. Now. Any ideas?"

"No. Not really." Leo pulled out his phone. "Dali might know though."

"Dali? Why would he know? Aren't you both relatively new to the pack?" Which would've been about a year ago, right after the pack showed up in New Orleans.

"Oh, no. Dali's Bandu's nephew. Didn't you know that?"

"Nope." Dax sped through a yellow light, heading back toward the plantation house.

"Yeah. Dali and I met at the restaurant we both worked at. He pulled me into the pack. He's been running with Bandu for years. Since right after his fifteenth birthday."

Perfect. "Okay. Give him a call. Let him know it's an emergency."

"On it." Leo whipped out his phone. A few texts later, he said, "Sorry, Dax. Bandu is out of pocket for the next few days. He has a thing tomorrow night."

Fuck. Tomorrow night? That was when the ritual was supposed to happen. Bile rose in the back of this throat. Had he thrown in with a pack that was involved in sacrifice rituals? It was starting to look that way. He swallowed hard.

"Dali says he can gather the pack if you need 'em. What's the emergency?"

Dax tightened his grip on the wheel.

"Dax? You okay? You look like you're going to vomit," Leo said, scooting to the far side of the seat.

"I'm fine. Tell Dali we're on the lookout for a gray wolf with one black- and one white-tipped ear who also has a white-tipped tail."

Leo sat there staring at Dax but didn't type in the message. Then he cleared his throat. "Why?"

"He's a suspect in the abduction of Pandora. He was spotted in the getaway car." When Leo didn't respond, Dax eyed him, noting the worry swimming in his dark gaze. "What is it? Do you recognize that description?" The shifter in question certainly wasn't Leo. Leo shifted into a pure black wolf with white paws. But it could actually be any number of wolves in the Crimson Valley pack as far as Dax knew. He had only run with Bandu and Leo. Dax didn't spend a lot of time in wolf form. Once a month was usually his limit unless he had to shift for work. A lot of the Crimson Valley wolves shifted daily and ran for pleasure. Dax was far too busy working.

Dax turned into the dirt driveway of the pack's main house. He stopped the Trooper but didn't kill the engine. "Well? Yes or no? Do you recognize that description?"

"Yeah, I do." Leo fidgeted and cut his gaze to the side of the large plantation home. "He's right there."

Dax peered through the windshield of the Trooper and spotted the wolf in question right away—dark gray, one white-tipped ear, one black-tipped, and a white-tipped tail. Dax ground his teeth together with the knowledge that his suspicion of the pack had just been confirmed.

"Damn," he muttered. "Who is it?"

Leo grimaced and said, "Dali."

"You're sure?" Dax asked, his eyebrows shooting up his forehead.

"Positive. Those markings are far too distinct." He closed his eyes and sucked in a deep breath. "But why would he take Pandora?"

"I'm sure Bandu ordered it." No one did anything in the pack without Bandu's go-ahead.

"But—" Leo punched the dash and let out a cry of frustration. Then he punched it again and sat there breathing heavily.

"Is there something else you want to tell me?" Dax asked.

"Cocksuckers!" Leo buried his face in his hands and shook his head. When he finally sat up and looked at Dax, he had a tortured expression on his face. "I signed up to help

people. Not be complicit in abductions. I thought we were
doing something good here. Are you sure about this? That
Bandu ordered it?"

"About eighty percent. All the facts line up," Dax said.
"What do you think? You know Dali better than I do. Can
you picture him abducting a vampire for no concrete
reason?"

"Yes." His response was immediate. "Dali hates vamps
just as much at Bandu does. If his uncle ordered it, he'd do it
no questions asked."

"That's what I thought. What about you, Leo? Would you
take orders without question?"

The younger shifter was silent for a few beats. Then he
gritted his teeth. "I guess the answer to that is yes. Because I
have. I trusted Dali. It's why when he asked me to start
something with those vamps at the gala, I didn't hesitate. He
said it was to show them we wouldn't put up with their
bullshit. Wanted to show dominance or some fucked-up shit
like that. I just went along with it, thinking he wanted them to
be wary of us if shit went down out on the streets. Then after
things started to get real, I looked to him for backup and he
was gone. But you stepped in, so I forgot all about it."

Dax recalled that Dali had just vanished into the crowd,
but everything had been so chaotic, he hadn't given it much
thought. But Leo was right, Dali had set him up. Probably
even told the vampires all that personal stuff about Leo's life
to keep him off his game. "Son of a bitch."

"You can say that again. And speaking of the bitch, there
he goes." Leo pointed at a silver Jeep that was pulling out of
the driveway. Dali had shifted back into human form and was
headed out of the compound by himself.

"Looks like we've got a shifter to tail," Dax said. "Ready

to find out where he's headed and what exactly he's up to?" With any luck, he'd lead them to Bandu. Or better yet Pandora or Willow and Talisen.

"I'm a thousand percent ready."

Dax grinned at him. "I like your enthusiasm, kid."

Chapter Eighteen

*E*adric and I crouched in the brushes, staking out the three-story Gothic-style house that looked like it had walked right off the pages of an Anne Rice novel. Link was beside me, already in wolf form, just waiting for my instructions. We'd arrived in the English Turn neighborhood well over two hours ago, and despite Allcot's desire to fly inside, ready to tear limb from limb, I'd persuaded him to do a little reconnaissance first. We'd circled the property a number of times, careful to keep our distance, and I'd noted every window and external door, making sure I had a decent lay of the land.

The biggest problem was that the house was huge. If Pandora was in there, we'd have no idea where to start. And judging by the steady stream of shady-looking shifters who'd been keeping guard all day, we'd have plenty of resistance on our hands.

"I think if we wait until after midnight, we'll have our

best shot of extracting her," I said. "We can take the guards out one by one, or at least try to, then make our way inside."

Allcot glared at me. "We don't even know if she's in there. I'm not waiting that long to find out."

"She's in there," I said. "There's no doubt."

"And how do you know that, Kilsen?" he asked in a harsh whisper. "All we've seen so far are shifters who look like they haven't bathed in two months and that piece-of-shit shifter leader Bandu. When I get my hands on him, I'll—"

"See that shifter standing on the porch?" I pointed and added, "He's got dark hair and a scratch across his face."

"Who the fuck cares?" Allcot was rapidly losing patience.

I couldn't say I blamed him. If I thought Willow was in there, I'd have been hard-pressed to keep from charging in as well. But we were only two people. Sure, a powerful vampire and a powerful witch, but by last count there were at least a dozen guards and who knew how many were inside. We'd seen enough come and go that it was impossible to tell.

"You should," I said. "He didn't have that wound when he walked in. Four scratches all lined up perfectly. You know where that type of wound comes from? One pissed-off vampire. I'd say Pandora is itching to hand them their asses just as soon as she gets a chance."

Eadric squinted, studying the shifter through the bushes. "I'll be damned."

"I daresay you already are," I said with a snicker.

He ignored me. "Fingernail scratches. And that's not the only wound he has either. Look at his neck."

My vision wasn't quite as good as Allcot's, but I could vaguely make out the red-tinged mark. "Fleur-de-lis. Pandora's cursed ring?" I guessed and squinted at a couple of other shifters who wore red nail marks. Now that I knew what to look for, they were easy to spot. The fleur-de-lis mark was on almost all of them, as if she'd purposely branded them all.

I grinned at him. "She'd holding her own."

"Of course she is." Allcot scoffed. "My Pandora doesn't take shit from low-life shifters."

"Or anyone else for that matter," I said, fueling his pride in the woman he loved.

He glanced at me, his eyes hooded. "You've got that right."

I chuckled. No one would ever accuse Pandora of being weak. "So, now that we know she's here and obviously holding her own, I think it makes sense to plan our attack for the least resistance. We could even call in backup," I added. "Your security crew."

Allcot shook his head. "No. They're tied up protecting the compound and everyone else who lives there."

"Right. Of course." I'd almost forgotten that Willow's nephew, Beau Junior, and his mom, Carrie, lived in the mansion. If not even Willow and Talisen were safe from this cult of crazies, who was to say the group wouldn't take Beau and Carrie as well? I considered calling Dax but decided against it. Not with the way we'd left things earlier. And not without knowing just how loyal he was to the pack. I wanted to trust him, but couldn't shake my lingering doubts. "All right. Just the two of us then. How do you want this to go down? I could go in first, be the distraction if anyone is awake while you search for her. Or we could both go in, guns blazing so to speak."

He glanced down at my ankle where I kept the tranq gun strapped under my jeans. "Does it work on shifters?"

"Work? Depends on what you mean by work," I said. "Most probably wouldn't survive the dose, though when I see Bandu, I think it's going to be hard to hold me back."

"You won't need it. I'll end him if he shows his face again," Allcot said with a snarl. "That bastard went way too far."

"He had help, you know," I said. "Carter Voelkel has his hands all over this."

"Voelkel. Don't worry. I have plans for him."

On the surface, Allcot's words were pretty innocuous for a pissed-off vampire, but his eerie, sinister tone was what sent a shudder through me. Dante had called Pandora crazy, but I could only imagine what Allcot would do if anything happened to her. Mass destruction came to mind.

Beside me, Allcot stiffened then his cold hand rested on the back of my neck, squeezing just enough to make me uncomfortable. Link jumped up and let out a low growl, warning Allcot. The vampire ignored him.

"What are you doing?" I demanded in a whisper, recognizing his action as a subtle threat. For what, I didn't know, but I wasn't having any of it. We'd formed a tentative partnership, but I wouldn't hesitate to walk if he overstepped my personal boundaries. "Remove your hand, or we're going to have a problem."

"Not until you tell me what your partner is doing here. If he was in on this from the beginning, I don't think I have to tell you he's a dead man."

"What? Dax is here?" I glanced around, my gaze searching each one of the shifters milling around out front. He was nowhere I could see him. "Where?"

"Behind us. His scent is making me nauseated."

I spun, twisting out of Allcot's grip, knowing he'd let me

go. If he'd been serious about holding me in place, I wouldn't have been able to move at all, at least not without breaking a sweat and casting a spell or two. It took me a moment of scanning the adjoining property, but then I spotted him. He was standing next to a large oak tree, watching us.

Our eyes met and he bowed his head slightly in what appeared to be a silent apology. A weight, which I hadn't even realized was there, lifted off my heart, and I sent him a slight smile as I raised my hand and gestured for him to join us.

Dax glanced behind him and made a gesture of his own. I stiffened. What the hell was this? Some sort of ambush? But when I saw Leo pop out from behind the tree and the pair of them started to make their way toward us, I blew out a breath and forced myself to relax.

Allcot was silent as he watched the two shifters approach, but his body was alive with destructive energy. I knew that if Dax or Leo said one wrong word, we were going to have a problem.

"Just hear them out," I whispered to him. "We don't know why they're here yet."

"Earlier in the day your boy toy seemed pretty loyal to that trash Bandu."

"Maybe he's had a change of heart," I said, praying that was true.

Dax stopped a few feet in front of us and whispered something to Leo. The young shifter took a step back, flanking Dax on his left. Link trotted over to him, sat down, and leaned into his leg.

"At least someone still trusts me," Dax said with a smile, patting Link's head.

"Is there a reason I shouldn't?" I asked him, crossing my

arms over my chest.

"No. But I do owe you an apology." Dax held my gaze. There was sincerity there and a hint of regret. "It turns out Bandu isn't exactly who I thought he was."

"No fucking kidding," Allcot said, his eyes blazing. "He's in there right now. Or did you already know that? Did he summon you? How did you find us?" Allcot turned his attention to me. "Did you tell him we'd be here?"

"No," I said, startled by his accusation. We'd been together all day. Surely he would've noticed if I'd contacted Dax. But the vampire wasn't his usual rational self, and that was completely understandable considering the circumstances.

I turned to Dax. "Exactly how *did* you find us?"

Dax jerked his head toward the round circular driveway. "See that Jeep over there?"

"Yeah." It had pulled in about ten minutes ago, but the shifter who'd been driving had been cloaked in a hoody. He'd been unidentifiable.

"It belongs to Dali, who just happens to be Bandu's nephew. I learned that today, by the way," Dax explained. "We followed him here after learning that Bandu was going to be out of pocket for the next few days." He glanced over his shoulder at the younger shifter. When he turned back around, he addressed Allcot. "This is Leo. He can confirm everything that happened at the gala was a setup."

Allcot swept his steely gaze over the kid. And when he spoke, his words were filled with venom. "You knew about this?"

"God no," Leo said, holding his hands up. "Nothing like that. I did not sign up for this bullshit. All I wanted to do was keep people safe. This…" He waved a hand at the house. "I don't know what that is, but abducting people, especially good people like Willow and Talisen, is unforgivable."

"Do you think Willow and Talisen are in there?" I asked, hope and skepticism warring for dominance in my mind. "Is that what you're saying?"

"We don't know," Dax said. "But we're pretty damn sure the abductions were coordinated. Here's what we do know: Dali asked Leo to start shit with the vampires then disappeared. Carter Voelkel turned himself into bait for you, and then he made damned sure you were able to find him even when he had the chance to escape. We learned today that Bella Jaxon is an eyewitness to Pandora's kidnapping."

Allcot nodded, confirming he'd already been aware of Bella's knowledge.

"From her description, Leo here was able to identify that wolf." Dax nodded again to the Jeep. "It's Dali, Bandu's nephew. Dali doesn't do anything without the go-ahead from Bandu."

"Yeah, he had me cause a distraction with those vamps at the gala, then he disappeared," Leo said, still vibrating with anger over the realization he'd been used. "If Dax hadn't been there to step in, I'd have gotten my ass kicked from here to Mississippi."

Allcot bared his fangs and took a step toward Leo.

The kid put his hands up again. "I didn't know what the distraction was for. I swear. Dax thinks Pandora's abduction was just a distraction to keep us from finding those two fae."

It was my theory as well. I met Dax's gaze and nodded. We were once again on the same page. "And if that's the case..." I trailed off, not sure I should voice my suspicions.

"It means the Crimson Valley pack is perfectly fine with the blood ritual that is supposed to happen on Asier," Dax said. "They are either part of the cult, or they are willing to sacrifice Willow and Tal in exchange for Pandora and the chance to wound Allcot."

Everyone was silent as we all stared at the Cryrique leader. Allcot's eyes blazed and he said, "If anything happens to Pandora, they'll all wish they'd never set foot in my city."

It wasn't a threat. It was just the truth. Allcot turned back to stare at the house again, and I cleared my throat before addressing Leo.

"So you realized Dali is in the inner circle and you followed him here," I said. "How did you find us?"

Dax's eyes gleamed. "Reconnaissance. And the fact that you chose the best place to watch the house without being seen. There's a reason we make a good team, Phoebs."

I chuckled and held my hand out to him. He took it and squeezed, then pulled me against his wide chest for a quick hug.

"We're going to find them. I promise," he whispered in my ear. "And bring Bandu and his thugs down in the process."

"Allcot has dibs on Carter," I said.

"He's welcome to him." Dax pulled back and smiled down at me. "Are we good?"

"Good." I nodded.

"Are you two done yet?" Allcot asked. "As touching as this little reunion is, Pandora is waiting."

I stepped back, my face burning with embarrassment. Of course Allcot was right and the fact that Dax and I had been anything except professional in front of him was unacceptable, not to mention humiliating.

Dax, on the other hand, seemed to not give a shit what Allcot thought and said, "We have a plan." He glanced at Leo. "Are you ready?"

The younger shifter nodded. "Yep. Let's do this."

Chapter Nineteen

"What plan?" Allcot demanded, his muscles twitching in agitation.

I tilted my head and stared up at Dax, waiting.

He winked at me and said, "Leo here is good friends with Dali. We're going to send him in first, let him get the intel we need, and then the four of us will decide the best way to take them all out."

I nodded. It was a good plan, especially if Leo was able to keep cool. "Are you up for this, Leo? Can you handle it?"

"Yes, ma'am," he said, standing tall. "The pack has been feeding us bullshit about being morally superior, and now look at them. The hypocrisy is disgusting. I won't stand for it."

I smiled at Dax. "Looks like you've found a passionate one."

"Most young shifters are. And when the rest of the pack finds out about this, there's going to be a massive revolt," Dax said.

"How do we know he won't warn them we're here?" Allcot asked, still staring at the house.

"Because they'll either kill him or lock him up if they find out he brought me here," Dax said. "And if they think for one minute he's working with you, it'll definitely be the end of him."

Leo swallowed.

I wrapped my hand around his upper arm and squeezed. "It'll be okay, Leo. We're here, and if anything goes off plan, we'll storm the mansion."

Allcot snorted his displeasure.

"Of course, some of us are ready to storm it now. So the sooner we get on with this, the better," I added.

Leo turned his attention to Dax. "I'll go in, take pictures if I can, and come right back out. Give me twenty minutes. If I don't return or text, come in after me."

"Ten minutes," Dax said. "And if there seems to be any unusual activity, we'll make a judgment call. Got it?"

Leo nodded and did a complicated hand clap with Dax. Then he slipped from our spot in the vegetation. It wasn't long before he was strolling up the front walk as if he owned the place. One of the guards stepped in his path, stopping him, and I sucked in a breath, holding it while I waited to see what would happen. But it wasn't long before the guard stepped aside and waved him in.

"Damn, he's pretty good at this," I said. "No nerves. He'd be a good recruit for the Void."

Dax nodded and draped his arm over my shoulders. "He has conviction, that's for sure."

I stared at his hand resting on my shoulder. While I knew we were crossing a line in our professional relationship, I didn't care. Not in that moment. I was coming to realize that

Dax was the one person I could truly count on, and it felt good to just have that connection.

A few minutes ticked by, and I started to get antsy. There was no reason for my unease. The guards were just standing around, unconcerned. Dax's phone hadn't buzzed. The house was quiet and no lights had gone on or off. Everything appeared to be just as it had been... until it wasn't.

Suddenly a piercing alarm went off in the house, lights flooded the grounds, and the guards shifted without warning.

"Fuck me," Dax said, already pulling his shirt off. He was going into full-on wolf mode. If he was going to battle the wolves already heading for us, he had no choice.

Allcot didn't hesitate. He flew through the air, more than ready to get down to business. Dax and Link followed, jumping from the vegetation at the same time. I, however, touched the sun pendant I wore around my neck, closed my eyes, and said, "Cloak me in darkness."

My palm started to burn where the small silver pendant touched my skin, and then suddenly the magic was crawling all over me as I gritted my teeth to endure the sting of it. The burning sensation intensified and ratcheted up to almost unbearable levels, and just when I didn't think I could endure it any longer, a sweet rush of coolness coated my skin.

I let out a long breath and stepped out of the brush, confident the wolves could no longer see me. The cloaking spell was something I'd recently discovered and was a useful one but not something I could use regularly since it didn't work on vampires. Vamps were creatures of the night—they could see right through it. But the wolves? They couldn't, and that made the spell perfect for our mission. I just hoped the house wasn't full of cult vampires, otherwise I was going to be screwed.

Either way, I'd deal with it.

The front lawn of the mansion was in utter chaos. Link was busy fighting off two shifters. Dax had his jaws around the neck of one and simultaneously used his back feet to kick out and fight off another. One was lying off to the side, breathing heavily with blood pooling around him. It was already a bloodbath, and the fight had barely started.

I walked silently through the carnage and right into the big house. Soft yellow light illuminated the deserted parlor, showing off the ornate, velvet sofa and armchairs. A large portrait of a vampire band hung above a fireplace. The only other decor was an abundance of white roses. Interesting.

A loud crash came from upstairs, followed by a scream.

Pandora. She was screaming for Allcot, panic in her tone.

I reached for my cursed dagger and ran. On my way up the stairs, I was almost bowled over by a wolf making a break for it. He had blood matted in his fur and panicked, wild eyes. I flattened myself against the wall and prayed he wouldn't feel me.

I was lucky. The shifter flew right on by, unaware I'd been right next to him.

The house was filled with battle cries, snarls, and crashing furniture, making it unnecessary to be quiet, and I ran full out, trying to find Leo and Pandora. Allcot could take care of himself.

At the top of the stairs, I paused and listened. Altercations were happening from both directions. Pandora's screams filled the hall, and I made my choice. I ran down the hall and burst into the nearest room.

My blood ran cold, and I froze in place, momentarily unsure of what to do.

Pandora hung in the middle of the room from iron chains

that were attached to her shackled wrists. Her T-shirt had been torn to shreds, and her skin was full of bite marks. That's what the shifters had been doing all day? Feeding from her? I wondered if they'd finally shackled her wrists because she'd taken to marring their sorry faces with her nails. She was paler than usual, and blood trickled down her arms and legs.

Allcot was near the window, savagely fighting four wolves. Blood had splattered on the walls and the ceiling.

But more importantly, Dali stood behind Pandora, holding a glowing stake to her back. I was certain, without a doubt, that it was spelled to mortally wound her, the type of spell that would take weeks before she died and cause unspeakable pain.

"Leave now, Allcot, or I'll kill your precious Pandora," the dark-haired shifter said.

Allcot's crazed eyes swept over him and the stake. Then her predicament seemed to sink in because he froze, still clutching the necks of two wolves. Immediately the other two rushed him, one of them getting him by the neck.

Fuck me. This was ugly.

A pleased smile spread over Dali's lips, and I realized then he hadn't just been following orders for his uncle. He was a willing, active participant who was getting off on Allcot and Pandora's pain.

Rage roared to life inside me, and with single-minded determination, I moved silently over to the shifter. I knew the moment he caught my scent because his hand tightened around the end of his stake and his eyes narrowed, scanning the room for me.

I struck and struck hard. My boot landed with a loud thud right in the middle of his chest. He'd been braced for a fight. That much was clear, as he only stumbled back a few feet, but it was enough to get the stake away from Pandora's back. I leaped in front of him, jabbing him with one fist and swiping my dagger at the hand holding the stake. My blade made impact, and he sucked in a sharp hiss.

"Bitch," he snarled, meeting my eyes.

"Douchebag." I glared back, not caring in the least that he'd seen past my spell. It had gotten me in the room, and that was enough.

He lunged, but I was ready for him. I struck out with my dagger, catching him in the shoulder. He howled and reeled back. Without hesitating, I stepped into him and landed a punch to his kidney. He jerked forward, head-butting me. Pain exploded over my eyes, and I lashed out with the dagger again, this time catching his other arm.

"You goddamned whore!" he yelled and threw himself at me, his stake coming right for my chest. I knew I couldn't survive an attack if he even nicked me with his weapon. I dove to the side, landed on the floor, and rolled, coming back onto my feet. Only he hadn't followed me—he was once again standing right behind Pandora, screaming we'd fucked up and it was her turn to die.

I ran forward, horror rippling through me, knowing there was no way I could reach him before the stake got her. In a panic, I called on the magic deep in my gut and imagined with everything I had that Dali was frozen in place. It was a Hail Mary, but it was something.

The spell shot from me in the form of a misty white cloud but wasn't fast enough. His arm was already in motion, the stake just a millisecond from piercing her skin.

I screamed, trying to stop the inevitable in any way I could, and just as the sound escaped from my mouth, suddenly a pure black wolf appeared from nowhere, his large paws knocking the stake from Dali's hands. The pair tumbled backward with Dali yelling obscenities and the black wolf dodging his blows until he got his jaws around Dali's neck and the man stilled.

"Eadric!" Pandora called out, her voice hoarse and full of exhaustion.

With Dali at least temporarily contained, I turned my attention to the three shifters still battling Allcot. He had his fingers around one's neck and was fighting the other two off with his free hand.

I reached down and grabbed the spelled stake Dali had finally dropped, shoved it in the holder on my tool belt, and flipped open the top of the ring I wore on my right index finger. Yellow pixie dust glittered in the artificial light. I dipped my pinky into the substance, dabbed it on the tip of my tongue, blew out a breath, and whispered, "Sleep, little wolves. Sleep."

The air in front of me turned gold, grew to a large bubble, then whipped around Allcot and the three wolves like a tiny tornado. The two wolves not in Allcot's grasp ceased to fight, and instead started to back up slowly, appearing confused. Then all at once the two wolves fell over while the other one went limp in Allcot's embrace.

Allcot stared at me, a scowl on his face. "You couldn't have done that sooner?"

"No, as a matter of fact, I couldn't. I'm actually surprised it worked on all three of them. It's not very potent. And it's very temporary. We only have—"

Allcot moved so fast to Pandora he was just a blur as he passed me.

"—a minute or so," I finished and walked over to where

the black wolf was still holding Dali by the neck. I knelt down and stared Dali in the eye. "It's a real shame you turned out to be such a piece of trash. Dax really liked you."

Dali snarled.

I tsked, shaking my head at him. "You don't scare me, you know." My statement was a lie. His dark eyes held so much hatred I actually shuddered. How did such a young soul end up with so much hate inside him? Knowing I didn't have much time, I pulled zip ties out of my pocket and secured them to his wrists and ankles. I looked at the black shifter. "You can let go now. They're the magical kind that will keep a shifter from shifting."

The black shifter let go of Dali's neck and backed up slowly. Dali thrashed on the floor, clearly trying to shift, but nothing happened. I gave him a cold smile and turned to find Allcot working to free Pandora from her shackles. He had a set of lockpicks but didn't seem to be making any headway.

Frustrated, he reached up and yanked. The chains didn't budge. Of course they didn't. If they could've been pulled from the ceiling, Pandora would've done it herself.

"Where's the key?" I asked Dali.

He curled his lip and shook his head. No surprise there. I hadn't actually been expecting him to answer me. I reached down, yanked his set of keys off his belt loop, and tossed them to Allcot. But just as Allcot caught the keys, I saw Dali glance over at a small table near the door. He quickly averted his gaze as if he didn't want anyone to know he'd been looking in that direction.

I scooted over to the table, reached into a small bowl, and came up with an old iron key. A slow smile claimed my lips as I walked over to Pandora and freed her. She let out a cry of relief and flung herself into Allcot's arms.

"Let's go," I said, noting that the three shifters I'd knocked out were already stirring.

Allcot pulled Pandora to the window and gestured for me to join them. I shook my head. "I need to make sure Dax and Link are okay first."

"I have to get her out of here," Allcot said, looking torn.

"Go." I glanced at the black wolf. "Leo and I will be fine." The wolf trotted up to me and bowed his head.

Allcot nodded once, and the pair of them disappeared out the window.

"Ready?" I said to Leo.

In answer, the wolf shot out the door and I followed.

Chapter Twenty

*T*he downstairs was pure carnage. Furniture was broken. Blood stained the white tiles. But there wasn't a shifter in sight. My gut clenched. It was far too quiet both inside and outside the house. Something was very wrong.

I paused at the door, listening.

Nothing. Nothing except the movement upstairs from the shifters we'd just battled.

Leo's ear twitched, and I knew he'd heard them too.

"Time to go. Whatever's out there, we'll deal with it." Steeling myself, I pulled the door open and followed Leo outside.

"Oh hell," I muttered.

Leo paused beside me as we both took in the scene. Six wolves plus Bandu had Dax and Link surrounded. Seven on two when everyone was a shifter was terrible odds.

"Welcome to the party, Kilsen," Bandu said without

looking at me. "You're just in time to see what happens to traitors."

Link growled and lunged for the pack leader, but Bandu struck out with an electrified rod, zapping Willow's wolf.

"You fucking piece of shit," I said, striding off the porch, my dagger in my hand. In that moment, I honestly didn't care if Bandu could survive my cursed blade. There was no mercy for a piece of shit who would zap a shih tzu, even if he was in wolf form. "Step away from Link, or I'm going to rip your head off."

Bandu ignored me and stalked up to Dax, his rod aimed at Dax's head. Dax held his ground, waiting for the precise moment to strike. I'd watched him take down many vampires using the same exact technique. If it'd just been him and Bandu, he likely would've been able to subdue the pack leader without even breaking a sweat. But with six other shifters rushing him, the task would've been damn near impossible. Instead, Dax met my gaze for one brief second then dropped to the ground and rolled.

I whipped out my sun agate and yelled, "*Siste!*" The spell was specifically for vampires and would knock them out for hours. On humans and shifters alike, it only worked for a short time.

The six wolves all froze, just as I expected them to. Luckily Link had leaped out of the way. He'd seen me use the agate enough times to know what it meant. But Bandu? He remained unaffected and took off after Dax.

"Damn." I glanced over at Leo. A sound from the porch drew his attention, and we both turned to see the remaining shifters filing out of the house. He let out a low growl, and darted after Bandu and Dax.

"Link, move it!" I called and took off down the street,

heading for Allcot's BMW, praying he hadn't left my ass behind. Dax was here, but I had no idea where he'd parked.

My feet had just hit the asphalt when suddenly someone grabbed my hair from behind.

"You're a troublesome witch, aren't you, Phoebe Kilsen?" The voice, full of hatred and self-righteousness, was unmistakable.

"And you're a dirty little wannabe hipster. Anyone ever tell you the girls aren't really into man buns?"

His grip tightened on my hair, and he yanked my head back. I winced.

"Shut up," he ordered.

Bandu started to drag me back to the house, but I braced my feet on the ground and reached back, shamelessly grabbing for his crotch. My fingers found a grip, and I squeezed as hard as I could.

He let out a howl so loud I was certain my hearing would never be the same. But worse, he didn't let go. He just fell to his knees, taking me with him.

"You'll pay for that, Kilsen," he wheezed out. "Do that again and I won't hesitate to snap your neck."

"You can try," I said, hatred seeping from my pores. "But I bet you'll lose that game." I jerked my head back, clocking him just above his eye.

"Fuck!" he cried, his grip loosening, but he still didn't let go. It didn't matter, it was enough. I jabbed an elbow into his gut and then flung myself forward, scrambling to get away from him. I was just about free when his hand clasped around my ankle and jerked me back. I fell face-first on the asphalt and gritted my teeth, praying I didn't have one hell of a road rash when this was over.

Unwilling to give in, I forced myself to flip over and

kicked my free leg out. I'd been aiming for his face, but I missed and got his shoulder instead. It was a lucky blow, because his grip faltered and I was free.

Within seconds I was on my feet, my dagger out. It would do no good to run. Wolves were faster than I was, and it was clear Bandu had no intention of letting me get away.

"You're really going to throw down with me, Kilsen?" he said, his face carefully arranged in an amused expression. But I saw right through him. He was afraid of me. Good. I liked it that way.

"Yeah. But don't worry, I'll make it quick. You won't have to suffer for too long. See, I'm not as vindictive as the rest of you assholes." I spun and jabbed at him, my dagger barely missing his neck.

He opened his mouth to speak, but before he could get the words out, another shifter came out of nowhere and knocked him on his ass.

I blinked and smiled when I recognized the gray-and-white wolf. It was rare for me to see Dax in his shifter form, but when I did, he never failed to impress. Then Allcot and Pandora where there. The four of us plus Link had Bandu surrounded. The only one missing was Leo. I glanced around, worried about the young shifter, but got distracted by the shadows moving toward us in the night.

"What the hell is that?" I asked no one in particular.

"Shit! She's coming," Pandora said, her voice panicked. "We have to get out of here."

"Who's coming?" I squinted into the darkness, trying to decide if the shadows were the shifters. No, that wasn't right. They were too big to be wolves, but not the right shape to be humans. I clutched my agate, preparing to flash them if for no other reason than just to see what we were up against.

"Let Bandu go," a raspy female voice said.

"Eadric, please," Pandora said.

I cut my gaze to the battered vampire and frowned. I'd never heard Pandora frightened before. Not like that.

"We're going, love," he said softly. "Just need to secure the shifter."

Bandu growled and dropped to all fours, quickly turning into a wolf. Link and Dax immediately attacked. Within seconds, they had him under their control.

I glanced over my shoulder at the shadows closing in on us. My skin started to prickle and my stomach turned. "What the hell is that?" I asked again.

"They're her demons," Pandora whispered.

"Demons?" Fear clouded my mind and I just stood there, staring like a fool. I'd heard of witches conjuring demons before, but in reality, I'd never encountered a witch so evil, so bereft of human decency, that she'd attempted it. Witches who summoned demons had to pay with their souls. And this one, she had an army. "We have to get out of here," I said, echoing Pandora. "Now."

"He's almost here," Allcot said.

"Who?" What the hell were we waiting for?

"Leo." He nodded over my shoulder, and that's when I spotted Dax's Trooper barreling down the road toward us. They'd sent the kid to get the truck while they helped save me from Bandu. And because we'd helped Allcot find Pandora, he was returning the favor.

The demons reached us just before the Trooper pulled to a stop. I raised my agate, flashing the brilliant light on them, praying the magic would do something, anything, to stop them.

Gut-wrenching screams filled the air, and all of them recoiled, backing up to hide behind their mistress.

"You dare to go up against my children?" she drawled, walking right into my light. It wasn't surprising that the agate didn't work on her. Similar ones didn't work on me either. But I was surprised to see her floating in the air, gliding toward us as if she were a spirit. Only she was just as solid as the rest of us. "That will not be tolerated."

"Get in the truck!" I yelled, moving in front of the sorceress, shielding them all from whatever she was getting ready to throw at us. I heard scrambling behind me and threw up a blocking spell just in time. The sorceress's curse broke my shield instantly, and a thick cloud of smoke rose up, obscuring my vision.

"Hurry," Pandora said right before she pushed me toward the Trooper. Another crack of magic filled the air, and a second later, I felt rather than saw Pandora stiffen. I spun, finding her frozen, her mouth open in shock, and she was floating slowly toward the sorceress.

"Pandora!" Allcot appeared beside her, his arms going around her, but as soon as they did, his flesh started to smoke. He jumped back, staring at the scorched areas of his flesh.

"Holy shit!" I turned back around and charged the other witch. "What the hell did you do to her?"

She didn't answer, but her demons once again started to close in on me. I flashed them again with my agate, and this time I noticed the light made the sorceress flinch as well. Not knowing what else to do, I rushed her, my agate shining bright in one hand and my cursed dagger in the other.

Dark magic poured from her fingertips, but thanks to the light from my agate, she couldn't see exactly where I was and the spell hit a nearby tree, causing a loud crack as the trunk split in two.

Another round of magic came at me, but I dodged and came up swinging, aiming for her heart. The blade slid easily into the sorceress, and I let out a triumphant grunt as the demons vanished. But the woman remained, her soulless black eyes boring into mine.

"You can't kill me, little witch. No one can." Then she wrapped her hand around mine and the hilt of my blade and pulled it right out of her chest, laughing maniacally as she tried to wrestle the blade from me. But there was no way in hell she was getting it from me. I lifted the agate and shone it right in her eyes as I shoved my boot into her stomach and sent her flying back into the street.

"Get Pandora in the Trooper," I ordered Allcot, tugging on the comatose vampire.

"She's still cursed," he hissed. "We have to get her to reverse it first."

"No we don't. With the help of a healer, we can fix this. Let's go before it gets worse." He glanced once at the sorceress already making her way toward us, then grabbed Pandora and shoved her in the Trooper, ignoring his burning flesh. I climbed in after them.

Leo stepped on the gas, the wheels of the Trooper squealing as he hightailed it out of there.

I sucked in a deep breath and glanced around at our battered party. Leo was driving. Dax was in the front seat, Allcot and Pandora in the back, me and Link in the middle row.

And trussed up at my feet was Bandu. A humorless, self-satisfied smile claimed my lips. His night was about to get a thousand times worse.

Chapter Twenty-One

*S*ilence filled the truck on the way back to Allcot's compound. We'd successfully completely our mission, but Pandora had barely made it out alive. And we still didn't have a clue where Willow and Talisen were being held.

A slow thrum of pressure had started to build over my left eye as fatigue set in. I hadn't slept in over thirty-six hours. Neither had Dax, I realized. I leaned my head against the cool glass and closed my eyes, seeking relief to my growing headache.

"Phoebe, wake up," a voice said from far away. "Come on. We need to get inside, and Pandora needs your help."

I jerked awake and blinked at Dax.

"Hey, sunshine. Welcome back," he said.

I glanced around the empty Trooper, then out the window at Allcot's mansion. "Eadric left his BMW back at that house."

"What?" He frowned at me.

"Allcot's car. He left it in English Turn."

"No he didn't." He pointed to the car in front of us. "We dropped him off and he drove it here. You were sleeping."

I blinked again. "Whoa. I was out."

He gave me a gentle smile and helped me out of the Trooper. "Come on, sleeping beauty. Time to get back to work. Pandora's waiting."

"Right." I scrambled out of the Trooper and followed Dax into the large mansion. I hadn't ever actually been inside this home. It was new. Allcot had gotten a larger place now that Carrie and Beau Junior had moved in so that they could have their own apartment. Considering his last place had been at least four times as large as the home I shared with Willow and Tal, I found it all rather extreme. But it also proved Allcot was at least generous if nothing else.

The entry was all white marble with a large crystal chandelier. Rare artwork from long-dead artists hung on the walls. Just in front of us there was a grand staircase, and to the left, the entry opened up into a formal sitting room. I glanced around, looking for the army of vampires that usually hung out in his place, and found no one. Where were they? Footsteps sounded at the top of the steps, and I glanced up to see Carrie rushing down the stairs. Speak of the devil, I thought.

"Phoebe, there you are," Carrie said, her eyebrows pinched together in worry. "They need you upstairs. Pandora—"

"I know. I'm coming." Exhaustion had set in, and despite my short nap on the way back into town, my limbs were heavy with fatigue and it felt like three flights of stairs rather than just one. By the time I made it to the top, I was winded and longing for a glass of water and a comfortable place to sit down.

"She's in here. The healer is waiting." Carrie pushed open a set of double doors and led us inside.

The large room was decorated with red silk and rich mahogany furniture. I knew right away it was Pandora's bedroom. She was lying on her bed, Allcot and his son David on one side and a woman with auburn hair piled haphazardly in a bun on the other side. She was wearing a robe as if someone had just dragged her from bed.

"Imogen, this is—" Carrie started.

"Phoebe," the woman finished for her. The healer rose from the bed and walked over to me, her blue eyes taking me in. "I wish it was under different circumstances, but it's nice to see you again, Miss Kilsen."

"Healer Imogen. I wasn't expecting to see you here at this late hour," I said.

She gave me a tight smile. "I could say the same to you."

Touché, I thought. "Sorry, didn't mean to offend. I was just surprised." When she didn't respond, I glanced over at Pandora. "How is she?"

"Cursed. Eadric said you were adamant that with a healer's help we could break the spell the sorceress put on her."

"Right." I produced my blade. "I have this. It's the sorceress's blood staining the tip. The only problem is my blade is laced with poison." With the right magical skills, we could use the sorceress's blood to reverse the curse, but the poison would be an issue.

"Damn," she muttered.

"I think we can still make it work though." I glanced around the room. "Can someone get us a bowl?"

"On it." David, Allcot's adopted son, rose from the bed and hurried from the room.

I walked over to Pandora and felt a rush of empathy as I watched Allcot tenderly wash the blood from her face, her neck, and her limbs. He whispered something to her the rest of us couldn't hear. I hoped she could, but there was no way to tell as she just lay there, motionless, staring at the red silk covering the canopy of her bed.

"Here," David said, popping up right beside me.

I smiled at the tall, handsome, dark-haired man. "Thanks."

"Not a problem." He walked over to where Carrie stood off to the side and slipped his arm around her waist. They'd started dating some months ago, and I was glad to see they still appeared to be happy.

Clutching the bowl, I slipped into Pandora's en suite bathroom and partially filled the bowl with water while Imogen eyed me curiously. I glanced at her and asked, "Do you have any dandelion root in your bag of tricks?"

"Sure." She disappeared back into the room and returned with a leather case of herbs. "Powder or leaf?"

"Powder."

She handed me a container of the herb, and I sprinkled it in the water. "I'm going to put the dagger in the water, but I need your help to separate the blood from the blade. Can you do that?"

She nodded. "Tell me when."

"When," I said and dipped the blade into the water.

Healer Imogen cupped her hands around the ceramic bowl and started to chant. Her magic rose up around us, and suddenly all the tension of the past two days seemed to drain from my body. There was just something about her power that was so soothing. No wonder she'd chosen to be a healer. I'd been passed out when she'd worked her magic on me the day before. Too bad, because her energy was divine. Strange, I thought. Hadn't I just gotten an uneasy vibe from her the day before? What had changed?

I watched as the blood separated from the blade and spiraled into a coil in the water and decided it didn't matter. Not now. I'd take whatever help we could get.

Imogen glanced up. "Now what?"

"We have to let the dandelion root cleanse the blood of the curse." I placed my hands over hers and let myself merge into her magical force. Our energies blended, and it was as if her magic was mine and mine was hers. It was a heady place to be.

"Phoebe?" she said on a whisper.

I glanced up to find her wincing and struggling to keep it together. "What's wrong?"

"The curse on your dagger. It's trying to probe my barriers, work its way inside me." She grimaced and gritted her teeth.

"Shit! Sorry." I closed my eyes and imagined the curse feeding back into me, rejoining with my magic where it belonged. Not with the healer and her pure energy. With mine and my already battered soul. The curse hung on to the sorceress's blood, clinging to it, trying to feed off the evil there, but I whispered, "Mine!"

The binding shattered, and the curse boomeranged right back into me. I let go of the bowl and stepped back. "The blood is pure now. You can use it to deconstruct the curse on Pandora."

She eyed me for a moment, concern radiating back at me. "But what about you?"

"What about me?" I asked, giving her a weak smile. "I can dispel it safely. It's not something you can do. Remember yesterday when I finished healing my leg?"

She nodded.

"It's basically the same thing. I've got this covered."

Imogen appeared skeptical but nodded and rushed back into the bedroom.

I sat down on the edge of the tub, pressed my hand to my heart, and focused on the curse strumming in my veins. Dispelling the curse wasn't nearly as simple as healing my wound had been. It had been concentrated in my tissue, not circulating in my body. But still, I had to try. If I let the curse remain, it would eat me alive.

Closing my eyes, I imagined a large diamond. In my mind, it shimmered under imaginary lights, twinkled like a beacon, called the curse to its sparkling facets. The curse burned as it ran through my veins, making its way to the diamond, its home where it belonged.

I gasped and clutched my chest, trying to ease the ache beneath my breastbone. I'm not sure how long I sat there as the burning slowly but surely concentrated in my chest. The ball of pain grew and grew and grew until finally I could barely breathe.

"Phoebe?"

It was Dax. But I couldn't talk. The spell lodged in my chest had cut off my airflow, and I started to gasp.

"Phoebe!" he said, alarmed. When I didn't answer, he ran back into the room, calling for Healer Imogen.

No, I tried to say. I couldn't let her work on this. It would taint her pure healer magic. She sat down next to me, but I flinched away, holding one hand up.

"Miss Kilsen, I can help," she said patiently.

I was sure she could, but I wouldn't let her. I shook my head and stood up. Something dislodged inside me and it was like a dam broke. Then suddenly the magic threatening to suffocate me burst from me and hit the large mirror with such force the entire thing shattered. My ears rang from the loud impact, and a couple of slivers of glass had lodged into my hands. I held them up, studying them, wondering if Healer Imogen was going to need to stitch me up again.

"Holy shit," she said from her place on the floor where she'd ducked down. "That was one hell of a curse."

I nodded my agreement and slid to the floor. Holding my hands out, I said, "Can you fix this?"

She was silent for a moment then very softly said, "Sure, Phoebe. Not a problem."

I rested my head back against the cabinet and closed my eyes while her lovely magic stitched the wounds in my hands, my neck, and my face back together. When she was done, she patted me on the arm.

"I think you'll live now," she said.

"Good. What about Pandora?"

Worry swam in her eyes as she said, "I think she's fine. She's awake and alert, but she's also nauseated and anxious."

"That's to be expected, right?" I said. "She was abducted and hit with a nasty curse."

"Yeah, I guess so. It's just that my magic usually solves all those minor side effects. I'm worried that if it didn't, I might not have gotten all of the curse."

I pushed myself up and held a hand out to her. "Let's go find out."

Once we were back at Pandora's side, I realized why Imogen was so worried. Pandora's normally flawless features look haggard. There were bags under her eyes and the wounds on her arms and legs were still prominent. She was a vampire. Her wounds should have healed almost instantly.

"Pandora," I said, sitting down next to her. "How are you feeling?"

"Better, exhausted. Still out of sorts," she said.

I touched her forehead and let out a soft curse. She was burning up, making her the only vampire in New Orleans who wasn't room temperature. I looked up and met Imogen's eyes. "She's still spelled by whatever that sorceress hit her with."

"But I... I could've sworn I got it all." She pressed her hand to her throat and closed her eyes. "I should try again."

"I don't think it will help," I said. "I think her body just needs to burn it off. She is a vampire after all. Immortal, remember?"

"Yes, but—"

Before she could get the words out, Pandora sat straight up then hopped out of bed. She opened her closet, revealing her vast supply of clothes, and said, "Get cleaned up. All of you. It's time to go get Willow and Talisen."

Chapter Twenty-Two

"Truss him up," Allcot ordered.

We were in a windowless room on the first floor of Allcot's home. The group of us stood in a circle, surrounding Bandu while two of Allcot's security team shackled the shifter and hung the chains from hooks in the ceiling, much like the pack leader had done to Pandora over the past thirty-six hours.

"Poetic justice," I said softly to Dax.

Pandora, who still wasn't one hundred percent healed but was looking noticeably better than she had back at the Gothic house where she'd been held, stood next to me and scoffed. "He deserves to have his dick cut off."

"After we interrogate him, love," Allcot said, brushing a long lock of her blond hair over her shoulder.

Dax and I shared a glance, and I took a small step away from Pandora, slightly unnerved by her vicious appetite for revenge. Not that the shifter didn't deserve what she had planned for him. It was just so... violent.

Leo stood across from us, his arms crossed over his chest, gaze fixated on the pack leader. Hatred and disappointment radiated from him in volumes. Healer Imogen, Link, and David filled out the circle, waiting for the interrogation to begin.

"All done, boss," one of Allcot's men said. "Need us to stick around for backup?"

"You can wait outside the door. Thank you, Harrison."

The giant dark-skinned man nodded once and slipped out of the room.

No one said a word as Pandora walked right up to the shifter and stared him in the eye. The low hum of the fluorescent lights illuminating the room filled the uncomfortable silence until Pandora unexpectedly spat on the shifter.

Bandu jerked his head back, startled, but didn't make a sound as the pink-tinged saliva trickled down his face.

"You will suffer for what you did. Do you understand what I'm telling you?"

Bandu's dark tortured eyes met hers and he said, "I already am."

She let out a humorless laugh then slapped him hard across the face. "You don't know what suffering is quite yet, but you will."

He was quiet this time and she took a step back. "Now," she said, her demeanor all business. "Where are Willow and Talisen?"

Bandu shook his head. "I don't know."

"He's lying," Leo said from the other side of the room. "He told Dali he'd be unavailable until late tomorrow night. Said he had something important to attend."

"Of course he is," Pandora agreed. "I overheard him talking about going to the ritual."

Allcot stepped into the circle and took his place beside Pandora. He eyed the shifter. "Would you like to start talking or move straight to the torture portion of this production?"

"What difference does it make?" Bandu asked. "It ends the same way, doesn't it?"

Allcot shot his hand out and grabbed Bandu by the throat. He didn't squeeze hard, just held Bandu's neck in his hand and moved the shifter's face back and forth as he studied him. "Do you think you're going to die tonight, shifter?"

"I don't think I will, I know I will," he said, meeting Allcot's gaze. "It's inevitable."

The two continued to stare each other down. Then Allcot let him go and said, "He's not going to tell us anything. This is a man prepared to die."

I had to agree. The shifter wasn't upset. He wasn't fighting or bargaining for his life. He was resigned. The question remained though—if Allcot tortured him, would he give up Carter Voelkel and the location of Willow and Tal? Maybe. But I had a better way.

I turned to Imogen. "You up for some more magic tonight?"

The healer blinked. "What's wrong? Is the curse still bothering you?"

"No, no. Nothing like that." I waved a hand at Bandu. "I can do a memory spell if I can siphon some of your power."

Her eyes widened, and she took a small step back. "I don't—"

"Yes, a memory spell," Pandora said. "Do it."

"I don't— That's not something I think I can do," she said.

"Sure you can, Imogen," Pandora said impatiently. "You owe us that much."

The healer frowned, clearly uneasy, but stepped up beside me anyway.

"What was that about?" I whispered to her.

She shook her head. "Let's just get this over with."

"If you're sure…" I pulled out a small vial of herbs that Willow had spelled for me not long ago. She had the ability to magically infuse plants and turn them into useful edibles. She made things like Mocha in Motion, a drink that refueled a person's energy, and Orange Influence, a substance that had the ability to control a person's will, though that one was highly controlled by the Arcane. But the herbs, they were a special concoction she made just for me for when it was absolutely necessary to interrogate someone—someone whom the Void would never get to talk. Someone like Bandu where the information meant life or death.

"She's sure," Pandora said. "What do you need?"

"Anyone have a mortar and pestle lying around?"

Imogen sighed. "I do." She turned and started walking toward the door.

"Wait," Pandora said as she pulled Allcot's phone out of his pocket. She texted in a message and a second later handed it back to him. "Someone will bring us one." Turning to Imogen, she added, "Work out the plan with Kilsen."

I frowned as I watched a silent exchange pass between them. Again, I wondered what was going on. What did Imogen owe them, and how had they managed to get her under their thumb? Resentment for the vampire couple, despite their help, curled up in a ball in my gut and sat there like a rock. Their contradictory actions never failed to piss me off. One minute they were helpful and the next they were forcing people to do shit against their will.

Vampires sucked.

"I assume you're going to use blood magic?" Imogen asked me, her arms crossed over her chest.

"Yes. But only his. What I need from you is a power boost. So that thing you did earlier when you helped to heal me?"

"Yeah."

"I'll need something like that. The herbs Willow infused for me are great, but they require a larger power boost than I can summon."

"Oh." Her arms fell to her sides and she relaxed. "Is that all?"

"That's all," I said, glad she seemed more at ease. If she'd been sure I was going to use her blood for the spell, that would explain some of her reluctance. Blood could be used for a lot of spells, most of them pretty nasty. And every witch I knew was extremely wary of letting their blood get into anyone's hands, much less a fellow witch.

The door opened and Harrison walked in with a ceramic mortar and pestle.

"Thank you," I said as he handed it to me.

"No problem, Phoebe." He winked and strode back out. Harrison had been one of Willow's bodyguards at one time. He'd proven to be a decent guy even though he worked for Allcot.

I walked over to Bandu and met his tired gaze. "This isn't going to feel good."

"I didn't expect it would," he rasped.

"There's one thing I don't get." I tapped his chest right

over his heart. "If you have such a hard-on for justice, why did you put your entire pack in danger? Why expose most of them to kidnapping and attempted murder charges? That holier-than-thou crap is really tired, Leader Bandu."

He sucked in a deep breath and glanced away, no longer willing to meet my eyes.

"Pathetic." Then, without warning, I jabbed my uncursed blade into his shoulder and twisted, sat down on the tile floor, and gestured for Imogen to join me.

He howled with pain and bucked, trying to jerk away from the knife, but it was no use. His wrists and ankles were bound. He wasn't going anywhere for the foreseeable future.

Imogen handed me the mortar without comment, and I held it up to the wound to collect his blood. When the trickle slowed, I twisted the knife harder and got a perverse pleasure in listening to his agony. Good—let him suffer.

Footsteps caught my attention, and as I was yanking the tip of the knife out of Bandu's flesh, Leo appeared in front of the shifter leader. There were tears standing in his innocent eyes as he clenched his fists and tightened his jaw. "Why, Bandu? That's all I want to know. Why?"

The leader slowly closed his eyes, his shame at being called to the carpet by one of his wolves appearing to break him.

"I thought you stood for something. You're just another liar. A user out to further your agenda," Leo continued. "You made me party to something that goes against everything I believe in. You make me sick." Leo started to walk away but then turned abruptly and rammed his fist into the leader's gut.

Bandu let out a whoosh of air and grunted but never said a word and never looked Leo in the eye.

When Leo returned to his spot in our makeshift circle, Link sat next to him and rested his big wolf head on Leo's knee. Leo glanced down at him and smiled. "Thanks, wolf. I needed that."

"He can stay silent, but he can't keep his secrets." I sprinkled a bit of the memory herbs into the mortar and sat down on the floor across from Imogen. "Ready?"

"Yeah."

I grabbed the pestle and mixed the herbs with Bandu's blood, then placed it between Imogen and me. Holding my hands out to her, I smiled. "Let's do this."

Her hands were warm in mine as I closed my eyes and called up my power. Hers instantly sprang to life, mixing with mine. I started to feel light-headed, almost drugged with the sensation. My skin tingled and my blood hummed.

Euphoria.

"Phoebe?" Her sweet voice filled my senses, only fueling my ecstasy, and when I opened my eyes the room was bright with brilliant white light and everything else had disappeared.

"Hey," I said.

Her lips curved into a shy smile. "Hey."

"This isn't so bad, is it?" I rubbed my thumbs over the backs of her hands, reveling in our joined energies.

She chuckled. "No, not at all, but..." Imogen glanced around the room, leaned in, and whispered, "But I think we might be putting on a bit of a show."

"We are?" I blinked. I saw nothing but Imogen and the brilliant white light. It was as if everyone had faded away.

"Yes, and they're getting a little impatient." She cut a sideways glance to where Pandora had been standing. "Allcot said we can get a room later."

I laughed. What was happening didn't have anything to

do with romance. It was… an intoxicating drug that took me out of the present and into a place I'd be happy to never leave. Except… Willow and Talisen needed me.

"Right," I said, focusing on her, then the mortar between us. "Let's finish the memory spell."

She nodded. I let go of one of her hands and dipped my fingers into Bandu's blood. Immediately the blood turned to a fine mist and rose up around us, obscuring her face from my view.

Then the scene opened up, revealing the memories for the entire room to see.

For me it was like I was plunged into an alternate reality and was standing off to the side as I watched Allcot and Pandora hand over a handful of drug bottles to Imogen. The memory was a surprise. I shouldn't have been in Imogen's memory, but I supposed our connection had been so strong that my curiosity about her had brought me to her memories first.

The three of them were in Allcot's office at the Red Door. Pandora was her usual sleek, sexy self, hanging on Allcot's arm while he peered at the healer. "These should help within the week. But you'll need to be available for the next month so the researcher can study your reaction."

"Can I work?" she asked, her voice heavy with fatigue. She had dark smudges under her eyes and looked like she hadn't slept in days.

"Yes. Just set up a schedule with the head of research. Some nights you'll have to stay here as your sleep patterns will be monitored."

"All right." Imogen stuffed unmarked pill bottles into her bag and turned to go.

"We'll help you kick this curse, Imogen. Don't worry. You'll be back to seeing patients in no time."

The scene shifted and it was another day. Imogen was in Allcot's office, beaming and shaking his hand. "I can't thank you enough, Eadric. I thought I'd never see the day I could practice healing again. Your drugs brought me back."

He nodded and made her sign a document that said she would be available for further testing until the drug was approved by the government.

Holy shit. That's why Imogen owed them. They'd found a drug to help kick a curse that she hadn't been able to heal herself—the kiss of death for a healer. If she was infected with a random curse that was zapping all her strength, she couldn't see patients and her livelihood would be threatened. The drugs must've worked, because the Imogen I knew was powerful and full of light.

And Allcot was responsible for bringing her back to life. Of course, now she owed them that life, which was no doubt why she was in her pajamas in their mansion in the middle of the night. They either had her on staff or were doing more testing.

Damn Allcot. Him and his drug company. There was no denying he was doing something great for the community with miracle drugs, but he was also a manipulative bastard. And that was the rub. He was neither all good nor all bad. The only question was did his good outweigh the bad?

Sitting on the floor in Allcot's house, basking in Imogen's beautiful power while we extracted a memory we needed to save Willow and Talisen, I was saying yes. Yes, his good outweighed his bad.

The scene shifted again, and this time I was where I was

supposed to be—in the purple Gothic house where Bandu had held Pandora.

The pack leader strode through the parlor on the main floor and into a library filled ceiling to floor with old leather-bound books.

"Is it done?" The raspy voice of the sorceress came from the corner of the room.

"Yes, Morena, the fairy and her spouse are being held at Mizer House until tomorrow night when we can complete the ritual," he said, not bothering to hide the disgust in his tone.

The sorceress uncurled from her position on the velvet chaise and floated over to him. As her scarred, distorted face came into the light, Bandu shrank back from her. "Your life is extended because of me, wolf. What do you think you'd look like if I hadn't given so much of my power to you?"

"Nothing," he said, staring out the window. "I'd be dust by now."

"That's right. You'd be ash and your pack wouldn't have their righteous leader to keep them on their moral path. Though I daresay the knowledge that you steal the youth of a fae or two every four years would make them rethink their loyalty, don't you?"

He spun around, hatred flashing in his eyes. "You're the devil."

"Not quite, my darling." She ran an arthritic finger along his jawline. "But close enough."

The scene distorted and when the mist parted, I found myself in the room where Willow was being held captive. Only she wasn't there. Not in this memory. The cell was empty and Bandu was pacing the floors. The redheaded vampire was sitting in a recliner, his left foot propped on his knee as he watched Bandu fidget with his keys.

"Calm down. I've got this covered," Carter said. "You need to relax."

"How can I relax when you're telling me our only option is to abduct the fae under Allcot's protection?" The shifter ran both hands through his dark hair. "This is going to blow up in our faces."

Carter rose from his chair and walked over to Bandu. He gently placed his hands on Bandu's cheeks, leaned in, and whispered, "You need to relax. I've got a plan to deal with him. All we need to do is keep him busy looking for that bitch Pandora and he won't give a shit about the fae. Pandora is his only weakness. We'll carry out the ritual, you and I will get another four years together, and our followers will become all the more dedicated. You know how powerful it is when the young ones think their souls are saved. Four years from now, we'll have an army of loyalists. Allcot will never survive this war."

"Only if we can get the city to believe his people are behind all the fabricated attacks," Bandu said.

"Oh, we will. Didn't I tell you? Five of the city council members have reached out to me after my invitation. They feel it's time to turn in order to have a fighting chance at pushing Allcot out of the city. I named my price and they gladly agreed. Once they get an indictment on the entire Cryrique organization and install me on his board of directors, we'll push him out and I'll be in charge of everything that bastard has built. Even if the charges never stick to Allcot, he'll be out of the city forever and the council will be in my pocket."

Bandu closed his eyes, clearly troubled by the plan.

"Come on, baby. You know this is how it has to be if we want to clean up this city. Make it safe for humans, shifters, and vampires alike. I know it seems unethical, but it's for the greater good. Once we get past this, we'll make a stronger, more equitable New Orleans. One where everyone matters. You're with me on this, right?"

"You know how I feel about the sanctity of life," Bandu said, trying to take a step back. "It's not right to take a life just so I can keep living a stolen one."

Carter let out a huff of frustration. "How many times have we been over this? Your life, the good you do, it's worth a hell of a lot more than two fae who do Allcot's bidding. You *care* about people. Not money. You make their lives better. You make *my* damned life better." Carter brushed his thumb over Bandu's cheekbone and leaned in, giving him a soft kiss. "Tell me you're with me on this, love. Say yes and I'll put it all in motion."

Bandu stared up at the tall redhead, eyes searching. "How are we going to keep Allcot from finding Pandora exactly?"

Carter's lips curved into something too sinister to be called a smile. "I summoned our sorceress, Morena. She helped us once, she'll help us again."

Bandu let out a tortured sigh and glanced away. Then when he turned his attention back to Carter, he returned the kiss and whispered, "Yes."

I glanced away, always a bit uncomfortable with public displays of affection, and found my eyes locking on someone spying on them through their window—someone I hadn't seen in eight years.

I let out an audible gasp.

Seth.

Chapter Twenty-Three

The visions cleared and I sat on Allcot's tile floor, stunned. The only thing I could focus on was Seth's face peering at Bandu and Carter through the window. What had he been doing there? Had I imagined it? Was he undercover, tracking their movements and trying to stop this just as much as we were? But if so, how come he'd been missing for so many years? The questions would not stop running through my head and I reached up, grabbing fistfuls of my hair, trying to stop my mind from spinning.

"Holy shit. I think we just entered the fourth dimension of crazy," Imogen said, her voice bringing me back to the matter at hand.

I glanced around the room, taking in the shocked expressions on everyone's faces. And it wasn't because they'd seen Seth. It was the insane plan of the shifter and his vampire lover that had them all frozen with shock. All of them but one.

Bandu.

His head was bowed and silent tears were streaming down his face.

"You're a disgrace," I said quietly.

The shifter nodded his agreement.

"Weak. Selfish. A complete and total fraud," I continued.

"People looked up to you," Leo called from across the room. "We believed we were called to be better people. But you... You used us, lied, and—" Leo shook his head, too outraged to continue.

Pandora moved slowly, taking her time, eyeing the trussed-up shifter. "So all that was to get to Willow and Talisen? I was just a distraction?"

The defeated shifter nodded.

"What a grave mistake you made, shifter," she hissed. "You and your vampire lover are both going to die tonight. And those plans you made, they'll die right along with you. By tomorrow morning, all your followers will know what a hypocrite you are. All that shit about how evil vampires are and this whole time you've been fucking a vampire of your own." She tsked. "Why is it always the hateful ones who are so hypocritical?"

Bandu didn't acknowledge her words. He just continued to stare at the ground, his tears falling.

"You make me sick." Then she reached down, grabbing my cursed blade off my belt. But before she could strike, Allcot was there, his hand wrapping around hers, stopping her fatal blow.

"Not yet, love," he whispered tenderly. "We need him a bit longer."

"Why?" she asked incredulously. "We know where Mizer House is."

I was glad someone did, because I'd never heard of it.

"The sorceress," he said. "They are connected. If we end him now, she'll end up here to avenge him, and we don't have time to deal with that just yet." He walked over and opened the door. "Harrison?"

"Yes, boss," the tall man said.

"I need you to gather a team and get this shifter down. Keep him restrained—he's highly dangerous. We're taking him with us. Got it?"

"Got it." Harrison pulled out his phone and began to punch in a message.

Allcot turned to us. "Be ready in ten minutes. We have a couple of fae to retrieve."

BY THE TIME we rolled up to Mizer House, I was convinced I'd hallucinated Seth's face in Bandu's memory. I'd asked Dax and Imogen if either of them had seen someone in the window, but neither had noticed. I'd decided I was half delirious with lack of sleep and was grateful when Imogen supplied me with an herb to keep me upright a little longer.

I glanced over at the French-inspired château as we rolled by and grimaced. Of course a shitty vampire would be holed up there with my best friend, waiting to sacrifice her for his lover's eternal life. Wolves couldn't be turned into vampires, so Carter had done what he had to in order for Bandu to live alongside him. If the pair hadn't resorted to killing innocent people to keep Bandu alive, I might've actually had sympathy for their situation. As it was, they could both burn in hell.

"What's the plan?" I asked Dax. He was driving the Trooper. I was in the passenger seat and Imogen, Leo, and Link were in the back seat. I'd wanted to leave Imogen back at the house, but she'd insisted she tag along just in case she was needed. Considering we were going to be trying to take down the one vampire that was immune to my cursed blade, she was probably right to insist on joining us. We were going to need her.

"Allcot's mission is to basically storm the castle," Dax said. "He's recruited about a half dozen of his vampires, all the daywalkers, to help us apprehend Carter."

"You mean take him out," I said.

"Yeah, that. He's just going to walk up to the door with Bandu and force Carter to open up. Considering all the lengths that vampire has gone to in order to keep Bandu on this earth, there is no way he's going to leave him on his own when Allcot has him. That will easily get us in the door."

"Seems risky," I said, already getting my blade and dagger ready.

"Got a better solution?" he asked, parking the Trooper four blocks away on another street.

"Nope. I'm ready to kick some serious vampire ass." I glanced back at Link. "Ready for Willow to come home?"

The wolf let out a high-pitched whine, and I took that as a yes.

"What's going to happen to Bandu?" Leo asked.

Dax and I shared a glance. Then I cleared my throat and said, "Allcot's going to end him."

"Not if I get to him first," Leo cried, then pushed the door open and jumped out of the vehicle.

"Damn," I muttered and slipped from the SUV. Dax and Link joined me. I poked my head back into the Trooper. "You gonna be okay in here?" I asked Imogen.

"Do I have a choice?" she said, obviously annoyed.

I let out a sad chuckle. "Of course you do. Eadric thinks

it's safer if you stay here. But then you'll be by yourself and…
Well, it's probably safer, but we never know for sure."

"Then I'm coming with you." She scrambled out. "I'm
not helpless, you know."

"No one thinks you are," Dax said, smiling at her. "Now
let's go get us a couple of fae."

Up ahead, I barely made out Leo as he leaped forward
and shifted into his wolf form. Then he was gone, off like a
rocket into the night. "Does he have any idea what he's
getting into?" I asked Dax.

My partner shook his head. "But we have to let him do
this. It's a terrible thing to have your idealism ripped from
you so suddenly. And, Phoebs, I gotta tell you, Bandu talked a
good game. I was even falling for his scheme."

"I know you thought he was a decent guy who only had
the pack's best interests at heart," I said diplomatically.

He snorted out a laugh. "You know, I think that's
probably true. It's too bad he was also willing to lie, cheat,
and murder to get the results he wanted. And damned if he
wasn't good at the lying." Dax shook his head and let out an
embarrassed laugh. "I didn't get to tell you. Earlier in the day,
he made me his beta. Wanted me to be his second-in-
command."

My eyes widened. "But he knew you were with the
Arcane. And you'd only been with the pack for a short time.
Was he serious?"

Dax shrugged one shoulder. "Yeah. He fed me a bunch of
bullshit, which I swallowed hook, line, and sinker, and I guess
he thought he had me completely snowed. I'm embarrassed
to admit that for a few hours there, he did. But then things
started to not add up, and that's how Leo and I ended up

following Dali out to English Turn. I guess you could say my Spidey-sense was tingling."

"I bet it was," I said, leaning into him and slipping my arm through his. "I'm sorry about our fight at the safe house. I just did what I had to do."

He paused and moved me to stand right in front of him. "You have nothing to apologize for. Your instincts were spot-on, as usual. I was the one who let my bias against Allcot get in the way."

I pressed one hand to his cheek and lifted up on my tiptoes to give him a soft kiss. "It's over. We're both back on the same team. Now let's go get my best friend and her husband out of there."

His dark eyes bored into mine for another moment.

Imogen cleared her throat. "Um guys, I think you might want to save the relationship talk for later. Because right now we have a problem."

I spun around, realizing we were only a few houses away from the French château–style mansion, and then spotted them. "Fuck. Can't we catch a break?"

"Not tonight," Dax said and dove forward, instantly shifting into wolf form just as Leo had done a few minutes earlier. He took off like a lightning bolt, and Link followed him.

I glanced at Imogen. "Ready to kick some demon ass?"

"As ready as I'll ever be."

"Good. 'Cause right about now, I'm really glad you didn't stay in that car." I grabbed her hand, tapped into her power, and poured every bit of raw magic I could muster at the dozen shadow demons headed straight for us.

Chapter Twenty-Four

*O*ur magic crackled and popped and sizzled as it bounced off the demon creatures surrounding us. They were on the short side, maybe five feet tall, wide set, big hands and feet, and oversized heads that had two rows of teeth both top and bottom in their disgusting maws.

If one of us was unlucky enough to be bitten, it could be fatal, though Imogen could probably survive with her healer magic. And if she got to the rest of us fast enough, we might be saved, but it wasn't something I wanted to risk. Instead, I continued to throw white-hot magic at them, battling away at their magical reserves. And when one broke through my magical assault and flew right toward me, I whipped my dagger out and prayed.

My trusty blade slid easily into the demon's torso. The demon instantly froze, and to my intense satisfaction, when I yanked the blade out, brilliant white light filled the demon and then exploded, annihilating the nasty thing from the earth.

"Fuck yes! Do that again," Imogen said.

I grinned at her. "That was a fair bit of luck, wouldn't you say?"

"Looked like skill from here," she said and jumped out of the way as another one came for us.

I lunged, getting this one in the back and laughed when it disappeared into thin air just like the first one. The rest of the demons let out a cry of frustration and turned, running in the opposite direction.

"No one can accuse them of being stupid," I said.

"True enough," Imogen agreed, her eyes narrowing as we closed in on the house. The demons had retreated, but they hadn't given up the fight. The ten that were left had doubled up and were going after Allcot's six backup vampires.

Since they were immortal, the demons' nasty poison most likely wouldn't kill them, but those jaws sure could do a number. Dark blood had started to stain the sidewalk in the dusky morning light, and if we didn't so something soon, the demons were just going to eat the vampires alive.

"Here, take this." I handed a sun-spelled stake to Imogen. "I think this will stop them in their tracks. It appears light is what they're most averse to."

She took the stake and nodded.

"You sure you're up for this?" I asked her.

Her eyes narrowed as she watched one of the demons go after Harrison, the same vampire who'd helped us earlier. "Damned straight." Then she took off, her stake raised.

I said a prayer that she had some sort of combat training and then sprinted to catch up and launched myself into the fray.

The fight was pure chaos. The vampires were at a disadvantage as there didn't appear to be any way for them to kill the demons. They weren't actually of this realm, and killing them seemed damned near impossible. The only thing that seemed to work was the light infused in my weapons. But getting the vampires to understand that while in the middle of a battle proved to be a challenge.

And because the demons had watched as I ghosted two of their own, none of them would come near either me or Imogen. I glanced at her, held up my blade and said, "Watch this."

Then I bolted to Harrison, who was holding one demon by the neck and trying to fight off two more with his free hand. I aimed for the one he had by the neck. With one stab of my dagger, the demon was toast.

Harrison stared at his empty hand for a half second, then reached for another one and held it out to me. I repeated the motion, and we killed two more before the rest of the demons realized what was going on and tried to flee. But it was too late. The vampires had caught on, and though they were bloody and battered, they kept the demons in place while Imogen and I finished them off.

When the last demon was gone, we stood in the middle of the vampires and took a bow.

"Thanks, boys," I said. "You made that really easy."

Harrison grinned at us. "Thank you. Now get in there and help Eadric find my girl Willow. You tell them that if anything's happened to her, they'll have hell to pay."

"About a dozen times over," I said to him, nodding. "Whistle if any more of those nasty creatures show up. Imogen and I have you covered."

Harrison gave us a mock salute and ushered us into the house.

I crept into the silent house, Imogen behind me, and strained to hear any sounds or movement.

Nothing.

I glanced back at Imogen, raising my eyebrows in question. She shook her head.

Okay. Think, Phoebe, I told myself. Where would a room with no windows be? The basement would've been my first choice, but New Orleans was at sea level and in some places slightly below. Any basement in a house in this town would be waterlogged. Middle of the house, maybe?

A crash came from upstairs, followed by a scream I'd recognize anywhere.

"Willow!" I cried and took off up the ornate staircase. As soon as we got to the top of the stairs, I slammed into an invisible wall and was thrown back. I bounced backward off the top step and let out a cry as I fell, tumbling down the stairs.

Pain blossomed in my left arm, and my head slammed into one of the stairs before I came to an abrupt stop. The world spun around me and my stomach rolled with nausea. "Fuck me," I said. "That shit hurt."

Imogen peered down at me. "Anything broken?"

I gingerly pushed myself up into a sitting position and realized I'd stopped about midway. Or, more accurately, Imogen had stopped me from rolling headfirst down the rest of the stairs with a freezing spell. "I don't think so," I said and took her hand as she helped me up. "Thanks."

"No problem. Want to tell me what happened up there?" She nodded to the top of the stairs.

"Barrier spell. I didn't see it and bounced right off."

"Morena's work?" she asked, referring to the sorceress.

"I think so." The idea that Morena could be upstairs

casting her spells on all the people I loved made my head ache with fear and pure rage. That bitch was going down, and if she'd hurt any of them, I'd kill her twice and three times on Sunday. "Come on. We have a barrier to shatter."

When Imogen and I got to the top of the stairs, I lifted my hand and pushed. Heat built and concentrated in my palm, then started to burn. I yanked my hand back and shook my head. Like a little heat shield was going to keep me out. I clutched the hilt of my dagger, raised it up, and glanced over at Imogen. She did the same with her stake, and I mouthed, *On three*.

She nodded, and after I mouthed the countdown, we both jabbed our weapons into the invisible wall.

Nothing happened. Nothing at all. Our weapons had pierced the wall but hadn't made a difference. I gritted my teeth and scowled.

"It's probably spelled to withstand those types of blows," Imogen whispered. "Try slashing."

I raised my eyebrows for just a moment then nodded. "Let's do it." This time I didn't bother to try to remain quiet. I just counted down, and on three we each attacked the wall with everything we had.

Slash. Slash. Slash.

Cracks started to form in the invisible fabric, lit up by the magic crackling over the surface.

"More!" I cried.

Slash. Slash. Slash.

A rumble that sounded a lot like thunder started to roll, and I intensified my attack. More cracks. More rumbling.

Boom!

The magical barrier shattered, sending flickers of light everywhere. Shouts and cries from a battle raging nearby assaulted my senses and I realized then the barrier hadn't just been keeping us out, it had silenced our friends too. I wasn't sure how I'd heard Willow cry out. Maybe she'd been trying to reach me with her mind. I didn't know and I didn't care. All that mattered was joining the fight.

I ran flat out again, already knowing there weren't any more magical barriers. Not with the noise coming from down the hall. Imogen was right behind me... until she wasn't. I was just about to burst through the door when I felt her sudden absence.

"Imogen?" I called, spinning around. My insides went cold as my eyes landed on the back of the redheaded vampire dragging her into a room at the other end of the hall. If Carter was down there, what was going on in the room right in front of me?

"Shit!" I couldn't leave Imogen to Carter's devices. There was no telling what he was up to. On the other hand, everything inside me said if I opened the door, I'd find Willow.

Gritting my teeth and praying Allcot, Dax, and Pandora had Willow covered, I took off down the hall and barreled into the room after Carter. And that's when I knew something was terribly wrong.

Chapter Twenty-Five

*M*y heart nearly stopped. Bandu was lying on the bed, blood smeared from the bite marks on his neck, apparently unconscious while Carter held the stake I'd given to Imogen at her throat. Two things were crystal clear in that moment. Carter wouldn't hesitate to kill her if she didn't do what he wanted. And if Carter had Bandu in this room and no one had come after them, then the people I loved most were in serious trouble.

"Heal him," Carter ordered her.

"I-I can't," she stammered, meeting my eyes, fear shining back at me.

Carter jabbed the stake at her neck, breaking the skin. She winced as he hissed, "I said, heal him."

I took two tentative steps, not sure if Carter had even noticed me. But if he hadn't, I didn't want to startle him.

"I'll try," Imogen said.

"You'd better do more than just try."

Imogen's eyes were still locked on mine when I nodded and mouthed, *Try. Try anything.*

She swallowed and laid her hands on the shifter's body. Light began to glow from her palms and spread over the limp shifter.

"Carter?" I said softly. "What happened to him?"

The vampire's eyes flashed as he glared at me. "Get out. Get out! Get the fuck out!"

I let my dagger fall to the floor and raised my hands in a surrender motion. "I can help her. With the two of us, the magic is more powerful."

He flicked his gaze from me to her and back again. "You're a liar."

I shook my head. "No, I'm not. At least not about this. We work well together. We got past the demons and the magical wall, didn't we?"

His eyebrows pinched together as if he wasn't quite sure what I was talking about, and then he jerked his head, indicating I should come forward. "If you try anything, I'll kill her on the spot."

"Understood." There was no doubt in my mind that he'd live up to that promise. The stake was hovering right over her carotid artery.

I stepped up to the bed, standing just across from Imogen. I placed my hands over hers and squeezed. Her magic rippled over my skin, and it was easy to see she wasn't even trying to heal the shifter. She was just sending light over him. I sent her a small smile, approving her thought process. If there was any opening, any opening at all, we might be able to stun the vampire with a blast of light. It was risky. Risky as hell to be sure since I already knew my sun agate hadn't stopped him. But I was sure a powerful blast from the two of us would at least knock him on his ass. Hopefully I wasn't wrong about that.

"It's not working," the vampire snapped. "If he dies, I'll rip both your heads off."

"How original," I muttered.

"Keep it up, Kilsen, and I'll take yours just for the fun of it."

"Nice pillow talk you have there, Carter. Is that how you bagged Bandu here?" I smiled sweetly at him as I called up my magic.

He scowled and said something about me being a first class bitch but clamped his mouth shut when he saw the magic sparking over my fingers. His eyes were glued to our hands, and armed with the knowledge he wouldn't hesitate to kill us both if Bandu died, I knew we had to try. I also knew that Imogen hadn't been lying when she said she couldn't heal him. Healers couldn't just fix blood loss. That required a transfusion. And since Bandu was a shifter, it required shifter blood. So if he lost too much blood from whatever had bitten him, and I was guessing it was one of the demons by the shape of the bite, he might already be a lost cause. But if we could breathe a little life into him, it would buy us time with Carter.

"Imogen," I said.

Her gaze flickered to mine. "Yeah?"

"Let's try a massive infusion of energy."

Doubt flickered over her face, but when I cut my gaze to Carter for a just a moment, she seemed to get my message. She nodded and sucked in a deep breath. Light glowed under her skin, and I was awed at the sight of her building her power.

She placed her hands flat over his chest, and I placed

mine over hers. And in the next moment, she unleashed her powerful healer magic. I sent mine, joining with her yet again, almost getting lost in the gorgeous beauty of her energy.

Goddamn, I thought. If this didn't bring him back, nothing would. Sweet, cool magic mixed with mine, fortifying it as I held it in my mind's eye and sent it all pumping into Bandu's chest. He lit up like a Christmas tree, nearly coming right off the bed. Both Imogen and I jumped back. Light continued to cling to him, flickering like twinkling lights all over his skin.

"What are you doing?" Carter roared at us. "Keep—"

Bandu suddenly sucked in a desperate breath, let it out, and then his chest began to rise and fall in a thready but rhythmic fashion.

"Oh my God. You're alive," he said, knocking Imogen out of the way and throwing his body over Bandu's.

Holy hellfire. Was Carter that big of an idiot? The answer appeared to be yes, because as I bent down to retrieve my dagger, Carter didn't move. He just held tight to his lover, fighting back tears.

I, however, was unmoved. Carter cared for no one but himself and Bandu. And even then, he cared more about having Bandu by his side than he did about Bandu's soul. It hadn't escaped my notice that while Bandu had ultimately gone along with Carter's plan, he'd done so to please Carter. The sacrifices, the lies, the corruption, it had been more than Bandu could shoulder. And while none of that let Bandu off the hook for his crimes, Carter was the one with no remorse, no moral compass, no empathy for anyone else.

And I was done. He would not live another day to order another sacrifice of an innocent soul.

"Say goodbye, Carter," I said.

"Not today, Kilsen." Like most vampires, Carter moved so fast he was barely a blur. One second he was lying on Bandu's chest and the next he was behind me, nearly breaking my wrists with his iron-vise grip. "Drop the dagger."

"No," I said, embracing my defiance.

His fingers squeezed and pain shot up my arm. I let out a cry as my knees tried to buckle from the agony, but I forced myself to stay upright and whipped my head back, catching him squarely in the nose. His bones made a nauseating crunching sound, and I knew I'd hit the bullseye.

"You fucking whore," he said and threw me to the side.

I stumbled, let myself fall, and rolled while Imogen let out something that sounded like a battle cry. When I scrambled back onto my feet, my eyes grew wide as I stared at Carter. The gold stake I'd given Imogen was lodged in his chest. He teetered back and forth, back and forth, then crashed backward, landing on his back, his unfocused eyes open and staring at the ceiling.

"Holy shit! How did you do that?"

"I just threw it." She shook her head. "I have no idea."

"I mean, what did you do to the stake? The last time I tried to dust his ass, it didn't work. He actually pulled my dagger right out of his chest and took off."

We both turned and stared at the statue-like vampire lying on the floor.

"I probably infused some of my magic, but I can't be sure," she said.

I shook my head in awed disbelief. "You're something else, Healer Imogen. You know that?" Then I grabbed her hand and tugged her from the room. "We'll celebrate this later. Right now we need to find out what's happening in that other room."

Our footsteps echoed in the hall, and I once again realized I couldn't hear our friends. I fully expected to run into another invisible wall, but we didn't. The door wasn't even locked. And when I burst in, it took me a moment to register the scene.

I paused, Imogen right behind me, and blinked, scanning the room.

"Nice of you to finally join us, witches," Morena drawled and then took a drag from the longest cigarette I'd ever seen. The thing must've been at least a foot long and smelled like cinnamon-coated tar. She was sitting in a recliner, her legs crossed while she drummed her scraggly nails on the armrest. Her hair was a tangled mess, her dress had moth holes, and her boots were coming apart at the seams. Morena, it appeared, was losing her hold on her place on earth. I suspected that if she didn't get her sacrifice, she'd be sent back to the hell she came from.

Wouldn't that be nice?

I coughed and scanned the room. Willow was in her cell, Link and Leo, both of them in wolf form, right next to her. Allcot and Pandora were trapped in some sort of shimmering bubble. Dax was pinned to the wall, held up by invisible restraints, and his mouth clamped shut. And Talisen was nowhere to be seen. I said a silent prayer he was safe somewhere in another room.

"You two owe me an army of demons," Morena said. "It seems you found a way to send them home without my permission."

"Send home." I scoffed. "Sure. If that's how you want to put it. You ready to join them?"

"As long as Bandu is alive, this plane will remain my home. There's nothing you can do to stop that," she said and pushed herself up out of the chair.

Power rolled off her in thick waves, making my skin itch. It was impressive really, the way she had Dax pinned and Allcot and Pandora caged and still possessed so much power I could practically see it.

"Come on, Morena," I said. "Carter is toast and Bandu is on his last breath, and your demons… Well, Imogen and I took care of them. Now how about you and me just finish this shit show?"

"That's a lie! Carter can't die," she screamed, her black eyes turning red with rage.

I suppressed a shudder and waved a hand at Imogen. "Seems all it took was a powerful healer. Check for yourself. He's a stone-cold corpse lying on the floor while Bandu struggles to breathe on the bed above him." I smiled sweetly at her. "I know it isn't the outcome you hoped for, but you fucked with the wrong witch."

She flew at me, her gnarled hands tangling in my hair.

"Son of a bitch! What are you, a thirteen-year-old girl?" I cried and twisted hard, cursing as she ripped away tufts of my hair. "For fuck's sake. Now I'm going to have to get my hair done."

Morena was not amused. The sorceress waved a hand and sent the recliner right at my head. I ducked just in time to keep it from knocking me out. I flattened myself to the floor, rolled twice, and scrambled to my feet, ready to fight, but as soon as I did, my eyes nearly bugged out of my head.

Bandu was standing in the middle of the room, holding the golden stake in one hand and a gold ring in the other. Anguished cries ripped from his throat as he held both in the air and shook his fists at the sky as if he was damning the powers that be.

Morena's eyes widened and filled with tears. Forgetting us, she flew to him and wrapped him in her arms, apologizing over and over and over again, telling him they'd be okay. If they stuck together, they'd find a way to honor Carter, to learn to love again.

Bandu stiffened, then pushed her away and shook his head violently. "He was the only man I ever loved. The only one I wanted to love. I've loved him for four centuries and these are the only things left of him." Bandu shouted angrily at Morena and thrust the ring her face. "Do you see this? The ring I gave him four hundred years ago. One of the cursed rings you sold us. The ones that bound us to you for forever. Now he's gone. And I can't even take mine off. You still own me, you wretched, horrible piece of evil!"

He dropped his head, his sobs wracking his body. Morena moved in again, trying to soothe him, but the moment her arms came around him, he jerked his arm up and the golden stake he still had in his hand went right through her heart.

She let out a startled gasp and whispered, "What did you do?"

Before he could answer, the light rippled beneath both of their skins, brightened, then exploded in a brilliant ray of light, ten times brighter than when Imogen and I had destroyed her demons.

I threw my arm over my eyes and jerked back, my ears ringing from the massive blast. For a moment, everything was silent. A reprieve from the chaos of the past few hours. But then everyone started to chatter, and strong arms engulfed me from behind.

"Dax," I said, resting my head against his strong chest.

"It took you guys long enough," he whispered in my ear.

I smiled, knowing he wasn't kidding. He'd known all along we'd show up, but no one could've predicted what happened with Bandu. I couldn't say I was surprised really. It was clear he hated what he'd become, and without Carter, he'd had no reason to keep living a tortured life.

"Phoebs!" Willow called from across the room. I glanced at the cell to find Allcot already picking the lock and grinned at her.

"Ready to go home?" I asked.

"Only once we find Talisen." Her voice cracked as much from worry as it did from fatigue. Her eyes were full of concern, and it was obvious she hadn't slept since she'd been abducted.

"Son of a… Dammit. I'll find him. Any ideas where to start?"

She pointed to a door on the other side of the room. "Try there."

"On it." I slipped away from Dax and moved to the door. Locked. It was annoying but not an issue. I dug into my pocket and pulled out my own set of picks. In less than ten seconds I had the door open and strode into the dark room. After running my hand over the wall, I finally found the light switch and flicked it on.

It took a moment for my vision to adjust, and when it did, I just stood there, frozen. Two cells were side by side. One held Talisen, and the other…

"Seth!" I screamed and ran over to the cell.

He sat straight up and blinked, much like I'd done just a moment ago. And when recognition dawned, a huge grin spread over his stubbled face. "Hey, sis. Long time no see."

Chapter Twenty-Six

*I*t'd been exactly three hours and forty-two minutes since I'd first spotted Seth sitting in that cell next to Talisen. In that time, I'd gotten exactly zero information from him on where he'd been the past eight years.

I sat at the kitchen table in the house I shared with Willow and Talisen, Dax on my right, Seth on my left. Willow and Talisen were across from us and Link was in shih tzu form on Willow's lap.

After Allcot had freed Willow from her cell and Talisen and Seth and I had joined everyone outside, Allcot had invited us all back to his mansion for brunch and some serious R and R. Imogen had taken him up on the offer, but the rest of us had declined. Willow needed to be in her space and, more importantly, sleep in her own bed with her husband. I, of course, hadn't any interest in staying at Allcot's house, though my opinion of him had softened some. And I just downright liked Pandora. She was a vampire with some serious sass and gumption. Definitely my kind of woman.

I took one look at Dax and practically ordered him to come home with me. After forty some odd hours of nonstop turmoil, I was ready to give in and take some comfort. I didn't know what that said about our relationship, but I knew he was the only one I wanted in my bed… whether the director liked it or not.

And that had left Leo the odd man out. He'd been living at the pack compound, but after everything he'd learned and done over the past few days, it was not a good idea to head back there, so Dax had thrust his keys at him and told him to stay at his apartment. He'd told him he could stay as long as he wanted because Dax was going to be with me. And that was cool… for now. We'd see.

"Anyone want more bacon?" Dax asked.

I raised my hand, feeling as if I was never going to get full again. Had I eaten at all? I couldn't remember.

Seth laughed. "For such a small girl, you were always one that could pack the food away."

I scoffed. "With you in the house, it was just self-preservation. Any food that was put on the table was gone within minutes."

"Fair enough." He winked at me and pushed his chair back as he stood. "Thanks for breakfast, Talisen. It was delicious. Best meal I've had in years."

Talisen raised one eyebrow. "You're welcome, but I'm questioning your meal choices since all I made was scrambled eggs and bacon."

Seth laughed. "I've been… out of pocket."

"I guess so." Talisen stood and snagged Seth's empty plate. He glanced at me. "Looks like we need to take your brother on a restaurant tour while he's in town."

"Sure," I said. "Just as soon as we find out how long he'll be here."

"Not long. I don't want to impose," Seth said.

"It's no imposition," Willow, Tal, and I said at the same time, then laughed. "Really," I finished "We don't have an extra room, but the couch is yours for as long as you want it."

"I appreciate that." He bowed his head in thanks and snagged the mug off the table. "I'm just going to grab a refill, then get that shower I've been dreaming about."

"You can use my bathroom," I called after him. "First bedroom on the right at the bottom of the stairs.

"Got it." He waved and disappeared down to the first floor.

I let out a slightly frustrated breath and glanced around, so grateful to have my chosen family back home safe and sound. I eyed Willow and Talisen. "You guys doing okay? Anything you need?"

"Just sleep," Willow said with a yawn.

"Okay, well—"

Willow put her hand up, stopping me. "Enough, Phoebs. We appreciate your taking care of us. And damn, everything you did over the past few days. You know I never doubted for a second you'd find us."

"That's because she's the best damned tracker at the Void," Dax said, covering my hand with his.

"Damn straight," I agreed with a grin. "Though I might've had a little help."

"Just a little," he said, grinning.

"Well," Willow said, humor in her tone. "Aren't you two cute. Is this a revival of that great affair y'all had a few months ago?"

"Wil!" I said, feigning offense.

"Yes," Dax said. "And as soon as her brother gets the heck out of her room, we're going to make it official."

Heat crawled up my neck, but I didn't deny his words.

Willow let out a cackle that actually turned into a yawn, and her eyes started to water.

"Okay, that's enough ribbing our friends about their relationship. Time for bed, Mrs. Kavanagh." Talisen held out his hand to his wife. And once she was tucked safely in his arm, he glanced back at us. "Remember, safety first."

Dax chortled. "On it."

The two fae rounded the corner, Link chasing after them, and a moment later, I heard their bedroom door close softly behind them.

Still chuckling from our exchange with Willow and Talisen, Dax helped me clean up. And when we were done, he led me downstairs. Seth was already curled up on the couch, his head buried under a blanket.

I eyed him, longing to talk to him. To finally get answers, but Dax tugged me into my bedroom, shut the door, and locked it behind us.

"We're going to need some privacy," he said.

One side of my mouth twisted into a smile. "Is that so?"

"It is. I have a lot of time to make up for." He backed me up against the wall and swept a lock of hair off my shoulder. "I'm going to need extra time to get reacquainted with every inch of you."

A shiver of desire tingled low in my belly, and I licked my lips in anticipation. "I think we're gonna need supplies for this."

A gleam of interest lit his dark eyes. "Supplies?"

"Yeah, you know, water, snacks, extra lube. We don't want to get dehydrated or weak or—"

"Dried out," he finished and dipped his lips to my neck, nipping gently at my delicate skin.

"Yeah, that," I said with a sigh, running my hand up the back of his shirt. He felt so damned good, his body pressing into mine, his lips tracing my skin, his hands digging into my hips. "Dammit, I want you, Dax."

"You've got me, Phoebs. In every way that matters."

I pulled back and met his heated gaze. Emotion and something that looked an awful lot like love stared back at me. His eyes softened as he studied me, and I could only imagine what he saw when he looked at me. Probably much the same, only I wasn't ready to go there. Not today. Not after such an emotionally charged weekend.

We needed time to process, to get to know each other, to just love each other in the moment.

I cupped his face with both hands and pressed up on my toes to kiss him. It was gentle at first, tender. Then he sucked in a sharp breath and deepened the kiss, taking it from sweet to hot and almost desperate in a matter of seconds. Our hands were everywhere, each of us fumbling with each other's clothes, tearing at each other, needing to feel skin on skin.

And finally, when we were free of our restraints, Dax stared down at me, his dark eyes molten with so much desire he made me quiver with anticipation.

"Now that you've got me here, Mr. Marrok, what do you plan to do with me?"

A slow, sexy as hell smile claimed his lips. Then he let out a growl and said, "Make every inch of you mine."

∾

I woke amid the darkness. Dax was beside me, warm and naked and perfect. I stared at him, remembering the way he felt hovering above me, pressing down into me, filling me, branding me with his hot kisses and staying true to his word when he said he'd make me his.

He'd succeeded. Because as I lay there in the darkness, running my fingers through his thick dark hair while he slept, there wasn't any other man I wanted beside me. Dax knew me. He understood me, and he for damn sure respected me. Add in hot sex and it was a combination I'd never be able to pass up.

I shifted forward, pressed a kiss to his lips, and then rolled out of bed. Then I threw on a fresh change of clothes and headed out to find my brother.

Seth wasn't on the couch. I glanced up at the clock. It was just past seven p.m. Had he slept most of the day like the rest of us? Or had he left? The thought sent me into a mild panic, and I took the stairs two at a time and rushed into the kitchen.

There he was, sitting at the table, munching on the largest sandwich I'd ever seen.

"Some things never change," I said, sitting down next to him and grabbing a chip from his plate.

He watched me munch and nodded. "It's true, some things never do."

"How'd you sleep?" I asked, not wanting to launch into the deep end of my questions right off the bat.

"Good. Comfy couch. *You?*" he asked, his voice inflecting a fair bit of innuendo.

"Perfect. Thank you." I got up and made myself a cup of tea. By the time I sat back down, I couldn't hold it in anymore. "Dammit, Seth. You have to tell me where you've been all these years. Undercover? Locked up? Amnesia?"

He let out a sad chuckle. "No. Those are all great theories though."

I slammed my mug down, not caring that the tea spilled all over the table. "I don't want to play this game. Do you have any idea how much pain I've been in? Or how long I looked for you? I just heard the other day that you'd been sighted a few times within the past couple of years. Do you have any idea how much that hurts? To know you've been out there and yet didn't come see me?"

"I did come to see you, Phoebs. I just…" He ran a hand through his thick dark hair. It was the same color as mine, only his had a curl to it I used to covet. Now I wanted to grab it and yank some sense into him.

"You just what, Seth? Just what!"

"It was too hard… I couldn't explain. It's…" He sighed. "I shouldn't be here."

"Of course you should. I'm you're sister. We're family." I placed my hand over his, and for the first time I noticed a platinum band on his ring finger. I stared at it, my heart nearly cracking in two. "You're married."

He nodded. "Listen, Phoebe. This is important."

I squeezed his fingers. "I'm listening."

"I don't belong here anymore. The only reason I came back was because I knew about the ritual—"

"You knew! And you didn't tell me? What the hell, Seth?"

"Phoebs, please. I don't have much time. I didn't know it would involve you or your friends. I had no idea about that. But I did know about Carter and Bandu. I've been trying to stop them for the past eight years. I failed the first two times, and then I'd say third time's a charm, but you were the one who made it happen. I just got captured."

I shrugged. "It happens to all of us at some point."

"True. But I'd been working this case for the better part of a decade. Not the best way to end your last mission, right?"

"Your last… What does that mean? You're leaving the Void?"

"I left a long time ago, Phoebs. Surely you knew that."

I shook my head. "Actually, I didn't know. All knew was that you were missing. Then I heard from some vamp that you hacked something for him, and I thought you were undercover. Didn't you just say you were working this case for eight years?"

"Independently. It was the one I wanted to finish." He cleared his throat. "Anyway, now I have and it's time for me to go back."

"Go back where?" I demanded in frustration.

"Home," he said simply. Then he stood and opened his arms wide. "Give your brother a hug, will ya?"

I practically threw myself into his arms, holding on tight as tears stung my eyes. We held on to each other for a long time, and when he finally pulled back, I noted he had tears in his eyes too. "I love you, Phoebs."

"I love you too, Seth. Please don't be a stranger."

He gave me a sad smile and turned and walked out of the kitchen.

"Seth!" I called after him. "Wait. I have something for you."

He paused at the bottom of the stairs, and I held up my hand in a wait motion as I hustled down the stairs and slipped into my room. It took me a moment to find the small photo album I'd kept for him just in case he resurfaced again someday. It was an album of the two of us, then pictures of me over the past eight years, documenting the milestones in my life.

I rushed out of my room, holding it up. "Found it."

Only Seth was nowhere to be seen, and the front door was cracked open. I ran outside and spotted him near a tree in the park across the street. Relief rushed through me with the knowledge that he hadn't just disappeared again as I stepped off the curb and headed toward him.

Seth glanced up, his brown eyes meeting mine just as I stepped onto the sidewalk.

"Hey, I found—"

"Goodbye, Phoebs." My long-lost brother sent me a sad, wistful smile, blew me a kiss, and with a *pop* he vanished into thin air.

Deanna's Book List

Pyper Rayne Novels:
Spirits, Stilettos, and a Silver Bustier
Spirits, Rock Stars, and a Midnight Chocolate Bar
Spirits, Beignets, and a Bayou Biker Gang
Spirits, Diamonds, and a Drive-thru Daiquiri Stand

Jade Calhoun Novels:
Haunted on Bourbon Street
Witches of Bourbon Street
Demons of Bourbon Street
Angels of Bourbon Street
Shadows of Bourbon Street
Incubus of Bourbon Street
Bewitched on Bourbon Street
Hexed on Bourbon Street

Last Witch Standing Novels:
Soulless at Sunset

Crescent City Fae Novels:
Influential Magic
Irresistible Magic
Intoxicating Magic

Witches of Keating Hollow Novels:
Soul of the Witch

Destiny Novels:
Defining Destiny
Accepting Fate

About the Author

New York Times and USA Today bestselling author, Deanna Chase, is a native Californian, transplanted to the slower paced lifestyle of southeastern Louisiana. When she isn't writing, she is often goofing off with her husband in New Orleans or playing with her two shih tzu dogs. For more information and updates on newest releases visit her website at deannachase.com.

74991150R00144

Made in the USA
Middletown, DE
01 June 2018